TWO CATS WALKING

Bettina Selby

Chivers Press • Thorndike Press
Bath, England Waterville, Maine USA

This Large Print edition is published by Chivers Press, England, and by Thorndike Press, USA.

Published in 2001 in the U.K. by arrangement with Mountain House Publishing.

Published in 2001 in the U.S. by arrangement with Mountain House Publishing.

U.K. Hardcover   ISBN 0–7540–4507–2   (Chivers Large Print)
U.K. Softcover   ISBN 0–7540–4508–0   (Camden Large Print)
U.S. Softcover   ISBN 0–7862–3346–X   (General Series Edition)

The text of this Large Print edition is unabridged.
Other aspects of the book may vary from the original edition.

Set in 16 pt. New Times Roman.

Printed in Great Britain on acid-free paper.

British Library Cataloguing in Publication Data available

Library of Congress Cataloging-in-Publication Data

Selby, Bettina.
    Two cats walking / Bettina Selby.
       p.   cm.
    ISBN 0–7862–3346–X (lg. print : sc : alk. paper)
    1. Cats—Fiction. 2. England—Fiction. 3. Large type books.
    I. Title.
    PR6069.E36 T87 2001
    823'.914—dc21   2001027305

For my grandaughter, Gabriela

CONTENTS

ACKNOWLEDGEMENTS

In the writing of this book we have received help and encouragement from many sources, not least from our house humans, Meg and Bill. Meg can be tiresome about sharing the writing machine which means we often have to burn the midnight oil and miss out on our beauty sleep. But we know she has faith in our undoubted talents, and moreover, she keeps a warm and comfortable house and always leaves her study door open for us. While Bill is often obtuse about our more subtle needs, he is a staunch supporter of our writing and has been generous in his praise, and unstinting in his efforts to bring our work to a wider audience.

Our thanks are also due to Jane Tatam, our editor, who has taken great pains to preserve the purity of our prose while dealing sympathetically with any infelicities in the script. Her skill and care has greatly helped, we feel, in producing a book worthy of us.

With Marieanne Griffiths, our illustrator, we share a mutual admiration. She has worked very hard to show us at our best, as well as to highlight our amazing adventures. And we have very much enjoyed having her undivided attention as she studied us. While we might look a trifle fat in some of the pictures, we have to remember that Marieanne is, of course, only human, and it is asking a lot even of so fine an artist to capture the true beauty and dignity of creatures as special as tabby cats.

The greatest thanks for the success of our Odyssey belong to Mimi. We love her to bits. Without her help our brave tale might well have had a very different ending.

Special thanks are also due to The Flock, current holders of the Golden Fleece who, as well as providing a warm shelter in an hour of need, also gave us the opportunity to win the prestigious Order of the Raised Paw.

We would also like to express our gratitude to all the creatures, seen and unseen, who eased our passage through Middle England. We think particularly of the gallant Champ who made us face a painful reality and of the kind owners of the mobile kitchen who gave us a much-needed meal in a lay-by.

Last of all we extend our thanks for all their kindness and support to Arnold and to all our feline friends of the internet, with whom one day we hope to create a world fit for cats to live in.

CHAPTER ONE

INTRODUCING US

We are Sappho and Dido, two cats who have decided to tell their story to the world.

The idea came to us because of the woman with whom we live. She is called Meg, and we began to notice that she spent a lot of her time tapping away on a machine and getting cross when we walked over the keyboard.

When we finally realized that Meg's tapping was to do with writing stories (apparently this is how she makes her living) we were very excited because cats are storytellers par excellence. We have been weavers of tales since the very beginning, long, long before

1

Homer immortalized Troy. In fact it was we cats who first gave Homer his ideas for Odysseus and the Trojan Wars. This, of course, was before humans lost the skill of communicating with other animals.

In the very far off days, before the Tower of Babel, all sensitive humans could learn from cats, and were very glad of their benign influence. But with the building of that tower the human race took a huge step backwards, and very soon discordant speech was replacing all the more subtle forms of communication. Humans could no longer understand the rest of the creation, let alone tap the rich store of feline wisdom. Indeed many cats would say that after Babel humans had the greatest difficulty even in understanding one another.

Only a very few humans escaped the general blight, but for a while at least, a thin scattering of kindred spirits, like Homer and the poetess Sappho (after whom, incidently, I am named) were able to maintain a link with the feline world. And it was into the ears of these humans, men and women upon whose shoulders had fallen the mantle of the story teller, that we cats were still able to breathe our secrets and our wisdom.

Once every praise singer, every troubadour and every teller of tales worthy of their calling was accompanied by a cat as they travelled the world, from palace to hall, hall to alehouse, alehouse to campfire, brightening the long winter evenings with tales of love and valour, of mystery and might.

Sceptics who question what I say need only reflect for a moment upon the exalted position that cats have occupied since the very dawn of history. Let them go to the Ancient Egyptian section of the British Museum and see for themselves in what deep respect and awe our feline ancestors were held. Cosseted, elevated to divine status, costly rings bedecked their ears and noses, precious gems and amulets of power were hung on silken cords about their necks. Their place was beside the throne. And when the time came for the pharaoh to lay aside the double crown of the Upper and the Lower Kingdoms, and to set out upon his long journey through the halls of death, at least one of our ancestors, mummified as he was himself, accompanied him to help decipher the sacred Map of the Dead, and to steer the astral ship on its course through the highways of the stars.

But enough of ancient history; back to the present.

If a mere woman could use this story-writing machine there was no reason why we cats should not do the same. Pencils and pens present certain difficulties, but we could happily tap away on the keys, telling our own unique tale for the benefit of anyone who cared to read it. And we would become famous.

So to begin.

We, Sappho and Dido, are sisters of the same litter. Our mother was a silver and black tabby with a lot of white about her belly—which is the part of her we remember best. Sometimes the memory of that blissful white milky softness and the lovely warm smell that spelt absolute comfort and safety quite over-powers us. Then we have to go upstairs to the sheepskin rug, to knead it with our paws and suck at the wool until we are sick, or until Meg comes and makes us stop. Meg does not understand the great poignancy of cat consciousness, particularly this kittenhood foretaste of heavenly delight. She is merely concerned that we are making brown stains on the sheepskin.

Fathers do not assume the same importance in feline family life as they do among humans, and so our Papa was not known to us personally. He is said to have been a huge black cat who terrorized the neighbourhood. Since there are few tomcats in the sparsely

4

populated part of rural England where we were born, the rumour is probably true. In further support of the notion is the fact that when Dido and I were fully grown, we too achieved a large and enviable size. Not fat of course, although some silly people have called us that. No, our build is more akin to the noble stature of our Egyptian ancestors.

We think we might once have actually encountered our Papa, face to face. This was when an enormous black male cat, with claws unsheathed and teeth bared, sprang out at us from behind the garden shed. We were still very young then; it was just before we were taken for our 'operation', and being particularly lithe and fleet of foot we were able to make our escape. Not that consanguinity would have posed any problems for cats in the direct and sacred Egyptian line, of course not, rather the reverse really. Ancient royal Egyptians liked to keep marriage within the family. We had fled because we didn't like being jumped at.

But all that came later. The first major upheaval in our young lives was leaving our mother and the first home we had ever known.

There were four of us kittens in the litter. I, Sappho, was the second born, coming after a big bumptious male kitten named Buster. He and I most closely resembled our mother in appearance, though Mama was forced to concede that my markings were more beautiful and regular than either hers or my brother's. I have four perfect snow white feet, a dazzlingly white bib and stomach and the longest of long white whiskers. My eyes are particularly fine, being very large and expressive and boldly outlined in black and silver. The rest of me is that perfection of antique silver and black markings known as tabby.

The third born was another female. She was black all over, which gives further credence to the idea of the fearsome black tom having sired us, otherwise she was unremarkable, save for being saddled with the unfortunate name of Serapina. She and my brother were never homed, but remained with my mother, part of an extraordinary bohemian menagerie of cats, dogs, ducks, birds and human children upon which our innocent blue eyes first opened.

Last of the litter, the runt, was another female, the one fated to be my companion, my sister Dido. She was tabby all over, but unlike my sumptuous black and silver stripes, hers were varying shades of brown and pewter, and the fur on her belly was a workaday beige. She was not blessed with any of my dazzling whiteness, except for the merest grubby smidgen under her chin. Nor has her fur ever assumed the exquisite silkiness of my coat, but is of a more woolly and coarse texture. We further differ in that the pads of her feet are a serviceable black, while mine are a delicate shell pink, requiring a great deal of attention to keep them in the immaculate condition required of our race.

The most striking and, to my mind, the most embarrassing aspect of my sister Dido's appearance is her eyes. These have remained perfectly round like those of a tiny kitten, giving her a permanently startled expression. Yet in spite of all these shortcomings there are humans perverse enough to admire Dido more than they do me. 'What marvellous markings she has,' they say, 'what amazing symmetry.' Meg even claims that Dido reminds her of a picture called *Tiger in a Tropical Storm (Surprised)* by a French artist named Douanier Rousseau.

After I discovered that Meg's writing machine also gave us access to the internet, I have used the facility to track down this Rousseau painting; it is in the National Gallery in London. Having seen it, I reject outright Meg's fanciful notion: my sister looks nothing like this rather crudely painted tiger except perhaps for the startled expression which I think of as Dido's daft look.

While I was still locked on to the National Gallery, however, Dido saw a picture which she thinks resembles her far more closely. This is an oil painting by Hogarth, and clearly the artist was a cat lover because, having been paid to produce a portrait of the Graham children, he made the focus of the picture an eager little tabby cat perched on a boy's shoulder. I have to admit that with its round eyes and big paws it does look very like Dido, especially when she is watching a squirrel or stalking a pheasant.

But enough about Dido's appearance. Back to the story.

When the time came for us kittens to go to a new home, it was natural that with my stunning good looks I should be the first chosen. This was when I first met Meg and her husband Bill. Actually, they are really William and Margaret, but humans have an irritating habit of tampering with perfectly good names. They meddle with our names too, calling us Sapphy, Sapph Sapph, Diddypuss, Diddy, and sometimes even Sapph and Did. So catching is this annoying habit that we even find ourselves using these unsuitable nicknames occasionally. When we were very young the gardener used to call us the Terrible Twins, but this insult we chose to ignore altogether.

Anyway, these two humans, Meg and Bill, were to be my new 'owners'. But when they came to fetch me they announced, quite unexpectedly, that they would take two of us kittens; 'company for one another' they said. Typical human fallacy this; in fact, once cats are fully grown they are solitary creatures who prefer their own company. You never see cats going about in great untidy gaggles like geese, cows, goats, dogs, wolves, sheep or humans themselves. Certainly not! But being both egocentric as well as decidedly anthropomorphic,

8

humans judge other creatures entirely by their own lights, and are therefore slow to observe such palpable facts. Meg and Bill having decided that cats need company, Dido had to come too. I think it was a toss up between her and the black female. On the whole, I am glad it was Dido, for it would have been very hard to have lived with a cat named Serapina.

My mother was casual about the parting. She had done her duty by us she said. We were both fit and well grown. She had trained us as best she could, and had passed on to us the basis of our race memory. It was up to us now. She only wished she could be shot of all four of us, as it was high time she got on with her own life. My sister and I were put into a basket and carried away to begin the next phase of our life.

Our new territory was excellent for young kittens. There was a large sheltered garden set on a south-facing slope with sun-baked terraces affording pleasant distant prospects. Smooth sloping lawns surrounded by shrubs and trees provided spaces where we could race around and pounce on things, trip each other up and roll over and over down the grassy banks. The house was good too, particularly the outside, which was covered in vines and roses. These climbing aids provided us with easy access to the expansive eccentric roof where there were further possibilities for exciting games. We played tag across the clattering tiles, we hid behind the chimney pots and balanced precariously along the roof ridges; while down below Meg and Bill wrung their hands, waiting for us to fall. Imagine, cats falling!

It was very hot and dry that first summer, and we spent all our days in the garden. We had hideouts in every tree, in the cool dark cotoneaster hedges, in the springy potentilla bushes and in all the many shrubs and flowers beds. A favourite game was pouncing on the butterflies and beetles that came to drink from the flowers on the bushes. It was our policy then to pounce on anything that moved; even if it was only leaves stirring in the breeze, we pounced on them. We also liked making tunnels through the middle of plants so as to be able to shoot out a paw at anything that passed—mainly at one another, but also at human ankles and wheelbarrows.

Our enemy, the gardener, complained that the place was beginning to look the worse for wear. But other cats and the more intelligent and discerning humans will realize from this account of our early play that we were being good diligent little kittens. They will appreciate that our games were all to do with the serious business of acquiring hunting skills. The gardener who thought we were 'little vandals' clearly knew nothing about feline development; no wonder, he only liked dogs.

Our main interest in humans at this stage of

our development was as providers of food and drink. We never came to them when they called us, for in the interest of training them to be good cat-carers, we did not choose to let them order us about. They could not reach us in the dense cotoneaster hedges, nor in the sprawling convoluted wisteria. We only let them know where we were for the pleasure of evading their efforts to catch us. They never could get anywhere near us unless we allowed them to.

Only at night did we permit ourselves to be bedded down safe and warm behind doors. Dido and I slept together on one big cushion, our arms around each other's necks. Meg and Bill took great delight in seeing us in this tender embrace; it confirmed their idea of cats needing company. We did not begrudge them their illusions, knowing that they would not last long. As soon as we were past our small kitten stage we would demand separate sleeping arrangements. But for the present we were still young enough to seek comfort where we could find it.

The humans, snug in their own bed were not around to notice how we twitched in our sleep and made occasional low moans. For the world transformed by night is a frightening place for young creatures. Like all cats we knew in our blood the language of the throbbing darkness. We shivered at the hoot of the hunting owls, at the sharp bark of foxes, at

11

the scurrying among dry leaves where the badger scraped with his terrible claws. Cats have a foot in both camps, in the tamed land and in the wilderness that lurks always beneath it. We can never belong entirely to the one or to the other. Night speaks to us in a wilder tongue, luring us from the warm hearth and the easy life, even as fear bids us hang back. Wrapped in one another's arms, sniffing the disturbing heady scents, we bided our time until we had grown powerful and cunning enough to be able to hold our own on the other side of the divide between the wilderness and the sown.

In those early days there was no doubting which of us was in charge—I, Sappho, the big sister, as Meg called me. First at the feeding bowl, I also led the games. It was I who chose the hiding places, decided which trees to climb and how far up them we would go. The garden was full of tall trees and, in most of them at one time or another, my little sister, Dido, managed to get herself stuck. I would be back on the ground ready for another challenge only to find that she was still high up, clinging to a branch, shivering and mewing plaintively, and back up I would race to rescue her. With patience and firmness I could always talk her down, and my humans admired me very much for this.

But sometimes, if I was a bit slow going to the rescue, or if I had decided that Dido needed to make the effort herself, Bill would get a ladder, climb up it, prise Dido off her branch, and carry her down struggling, scratching and mewling pathetically. I could have told Bill that this was not the right way to treat a sensitive cat. But of course humans don't know how to listen; as I wrote earlier, they lost the art when they built the Tower of Babel. Very few of them have anything more than basic language skills now; and most are cut off entirely from subtle thought and intercourse, even on as basic a level as this. Bill is no exception. He is a good man on the whole but suffers from the usual inadequacies of humans.

While on the subject of human inadequacy, not to mention downright insensitivity, I must cite the extraordinarily obtuse decision of Meg and Bill's in inviting my sister and myself to share their home in the first place. They had absolutely no right to do such a thing as they already had a cat living with them, a fine elegant town cat called Sedgewick who, at the advanced age of sixteen and a half years, welcomed his territory being invaded by two active young kittens as much as he would have enjoyed a cold dousing with a hosepipe! In fact it was much the same really. But of course Meg and Bill would never have thought to consult Sedgewick's feelings on the matter first.

Actually, when I say Sedgewick was elegant,

what I mean is that to a cat's discerning eye it was plain to see how very suave and debonair he must once have been; which was of course the reason he had been named Sedgewick—after something in the city he thought, a financier or a treasury official possibly. But when our paths met Sedgewick was well past his prime. His coat was already beginning to fade from rich sable to dingy brown. There were many grey flecks around his head, and he was as light and as sere as a reed. He was visibly fading away and most of the time he slept.

This venerable and dignified Sedgewick had not long before been wrenched away from his familiar life about town and from his established territory and lifelong associates, because Meg and Bill had taken it into their heads to retire to a rural setting. After being subjected to the upheaval of having his home dismantled around him, and to a most terrifying journey in a motor car, Sedgewick had been thrust, without ceremony or preparation, into the alien world of a country cottage.

Incidentally, immediately on arrival there, Sedgewick was accosted by a fearsome black cat whom we feel could have been none other than our Papa. Apparently the encounter had left Sedgewick so panic stricken that he was holed up for hours beneath a dense laurel hedge. He had not dared to answer Meg's calls for fear the monster would return and kill him.

So noble and forgiving a nature did the fine old Sedgewick possess, however, that in spite of the awful indignity of the move, the grief of his exile and the terrifying encounter with our Papa, he was prepared to adapt to the new and alien terrain, and to try and live out his final brief span in cordial friendship with his humans. It was then that they dealt him this further crippling blow of introducing, not one, but two young bouncing kittens to shatter his hard-won tranquillity. Possibly they might have had some idea that our arrival would rejuvenate him, 'warm him up' as Abishag the Shunamite girl was supposed to do for King David when he was old and dying and 'gat no heat'. Sedgewick, being a neutered male, certainly did not view our advent in this light but, as he subsequently taught us, the most important maxim when dealing with one's people is to 'Remember that they are only human'.

Had we been less well-mannered kittens Sedgewick would doubtless have suffered more. As it was we treated him with great deference—for a while anyway. We did not dare to eat from his bowl, nor to join in when he demanded offerings of food from Meg and Bill lunching in the garden. When he cuffed us or hissed menacingly at our approach, we meekly bowed our heads and made no move to retaliate. He did not really bother us much for, as I said, he mostly spent his days sleeping in the garden where he chose the dampest gloomiest spots in order to make his humans feel guilty.

Our patience and forbearance were finally rewarded, for slowly Sedgewick grew more tolerant of us, accepting first Dido, and then me. I suppose being the dominant kitten I was more of a threat to his authority, whereas Dido with her daft look was seldom taken completely seriously. But the real breakthrough in our relationship with Sedgewick came about through our shrew games. We don't eat shrews, they taste horrid. Mice of course are quite a different matter, and we devour them with pleasure, wasting nothing except for that tiny bitter piece of gut, which we usually leave as a trophy for Meg to find.

Shrews, however, possess one characteristic that makes them worth the catching—they can be made to run around in circles like toy trains. There are hundreds of shrews in these parts, though Meg insists that they are a protected species, and we have to be careful to play this game when she is not around or she will make us let the shrew escape. As Sedgewick was soon to teach us, there is no understanding the ways of humans!

Well, anyway, we were playing 'shrew trains' one day when we noticed that Sedgewick was watching us intently. We turned our backs so that he could continue to watch without losing face, but we could sense he was becoming most excited, just as if he was a young kitten again. He had never seen a shrew in the city, though he knew far more than we did about foxes, having once had a vixen rear her cubs at the end of his small town garden. After his first experience of shrew trains he often wanted to play too, and we always let him. In return he stopped spitting at us and began telling us stories about his past life. He also started sleeping in sunnier parts of the garden which greatly pleased the humans.

Our lives might well have continued in this pleasant uneventful way, and we would have had a very different tale to tell, had it not been for Dido, or rather for Dido's predilection for crossing the road.

Meg had already taken against this road. She said it was the one fly in the ointment of their rural idyll. The road was very steep and had many bends in it. In the sharpest of them nestled the cottage, a flight of rustic stone steps rising up to it through the steep front garden, which was a riot of roses and flowering shrubs. A lovely setting certainly, and tourists were always stopping to admire the 'chocolate box of a cottage' as they called it. The remarks pleased our humans very much—humans like having their possessions admired—but every machine coming up the hill revved its engine and changed gear with a great cacophony of sound just outside the cottage. Vehicles going fast downhill did so with a great squealing of brakes and tyres as they struggled with the bend, the steepness of which always seemed to catch them by surprise. Not all cars did take this corner successfully and several accidents occurred there.

At weekends the traffic was mostly holiday people going to the seaside for the day. They returned at dusk wearing very few clothes and with their skins all red and shiny. Usually the windows and sometimes the roofs of the cars would be open, and loud thumping music would pour out. Sometimes bottles came out too and tins and paper bags. Sedgewick, who was sensible about roads, would take an evening stroll by the hedgerows after the motorists had all gone. He said the bags and the shiny trays that had come out of the cars had interesting bits of food in them with smells he remembered from his London days.

During the week most of the vehicles using the hill were bigger and noisier, and ground their way up past our cottage with considerably more effort than the music-making cars. One of our front garden games was to see how long we could bear the roar of the great crane rumbling around the bend before we had to run for cover. The crane came every week day, as did huge tractors carrying grain from the fields along the valley bottom to the silo at the top of the hill. The din of these huge machines as they revved their engines and changed gear on the last slope always proved too much for us. We could never quite wait until they drew level. Only Sedgewick managed to stand his ground and that was because he had begun to grow very deaf.

But I cannot say the traffic upset us unduly; Dido and I could always retreat to the main garden at the rear of the house or into the fields beyond. Like all cats we are able to ignore what we don't like. It was Meg tapping away on her writing machine who was driven demented by the noise. 'How can anyone think, leave alone write in this racket?' she would moan to Bill. 'We came to the country to escape from traffic, but this is far worse than anything we had to put up with in London.' Bill's face would take on its closed stubborn look and he would say 'Well I for one am not moving again, ever!'

But that was before the day Dido took it into her head to extend her territory to include the land on the other side of the road, where a dense belt of trees offered good hunting. Unlike Sedgewick, Dido had no sense at all where roads were concerned. Time and time again she was observed skipping across the tarmac, airily ignoring the cars and lorries, missing death by inches. And after the humans had seen her doing this a few times Bill's attitude changed. Now when Meg held her head and complained about the traffic noise, he no longer looked cross, but encouraged her in talk of moving.

At this stage of our lives we did not realize what moving meant, and fortunately for Sedgewick, he, by this time, had grown far too deaf to overhear our humans' plans.

CHAPTER TWO

MOVING

Humans always complain about moving house. 'Absolute hell' we have heard them call it. Well, we just wish they could have even the smallest idea of what moving means to their cats; then they really would have some knowledge of the nether regions.

The reason that moving house is so much worse for cats should be obvious even to the least perceptive of humans. Chiefly, of course, it is because of the life and death importance that the home base has for all felines. Humans who make a study of animal behaviour have concluded that most of a cat's brain is taken up with making continual minute adjustments to an internalized map of its territory. They say a cat who strays or who is taken out of the area covered by this internal map is totally lost, unable to find her way home again. Reintroduced, even to the extreme fringes of a territory she once knew, they say, and 'hey presto' instantly the cat will remember all of it, even if the break from it has been a long one.

This statement, of course, is essentially nonsense! Scientists are always imagining they can fathom the intelligences of other creatures when they have only the dimmest idea of how their own species functions. The truth is that most of a cat's vast and subtle brain is a closed book to human scientists; it contains knowledge far too advanced for such newly evolved creatures as *homo sapiens* to begin to comprehend. However, with regard to the importance of territory in the daily life of a cat, they have hit upon a partial truth.

Apart from a few feline exceptions, unnatural cats cursed with a wanderlust, such as Dick Whittington's companion, or the cats who helped Christopher Columbus with his navigations in the Pacific Ocean, travelled the Silk Road with Marco Polo and accompanied other misguided but notable explorers through the jungles and deserts of the unknown regions, we cats prefer a detailed knowledge of the area of the world we live in, rather than a smattering of superficial details about far-ranging passages through the farther reaches of the planet.

This is just good sense, of course, for to have an intimate knowledge of our immediate sphere of operations is the best way to ensure survival. For small creatures such as us, danger lurks everywhere, and everything and everyone is a potential hazard. We must therefore treat all things and all places with caution until we are assured they are harmless. To anticipate where danger might be lurking is the key to avoiding trouble and preserving dignity. Apart from mere survival, no cat enjoys ignominious flight.

Comfort is equally important for felines. Ease, luxury and contentment are all essential for a full enjoyment of life, and such benefits are not simply handed to us on a plate. They all require a great deal of painstaking territorial exploration and research on our part. After securing our food supplies, by far the most critical aspect of this research is finding the warmest, cosiest, securest spots, both inside and out, in which to sleep without fear of disturbance. Sleep in cats is not as we once conveyed to Shakespeare, to 'knit up the ravelled sleave of care'. Not at all. That kind of sleep is purely for humans. Cats don't go in for care: we do not believe in it.

For cats, sleep is either pure pleasure or a time of learning. We do a lot of what humans might call dreaming, but which we know as tuning-in. It is how we retrace our way back through the accumulated experiences of our race. How we gain access to the knowledge and wisdom that is the basis of the task apportioned to us from the beginning. 'The cats' burden' you could call it though 'sacred duty' is how we think of it. The role of cats in the business of maintaining the creation has seldom been guessed at by lesser beings, and never appreciated at all by humans, not even I suspect by those who most admire us. The Ancient Egyptians were a notable exception in that they realized something of our worth. Not all of it of course; for perceptive though they were, they too were merely human.

The truth is, that without us cats and our sustaining influence upon the human population, life on this planet would fall apart. There are even some who think that if cats lost their power the whole universe would most probably founder. We personally consider this is too big a claim. But whether it is or not, clearly our well-being is of paramount importance to us and to the world in general. It certainly cannot be left to the inadequate provision of humans.

We require literally scores of different places for our tuning-in, each one suitable for a particular time and a particular set of circumstances. Considerations like wind direction, position of the sun, state of the fire, draughts, level of sound, all must be taken into account. Not to mention that indefinable difference, that communion with subtle matter, of which only cats can be fully aware.

Dido and I have always been properly diligent in searching out suitable indoor resting places. Although we are not averse to sharing a well-padded armchair with our humans occasionally, we operate best in small, enclosed spaces, ones that remind us of the secret hidden tombs in the heart of the pyramids, or the priests' chambers beneath the altars of Delphic oracles in Ancient Greece— places where ultimate secrets were unravelled and riddles made plain. Any open drawer or cupboard can provide opportunities for several hours of fruitful undisturbed reverie. Unfortunately, our zeal for finding suitable places often leads to our being incarcerated for far longer periods than we had intended. Meg and Bill have never learnt not to close a door or to shut a drawer without first checking to see if one or other of us is behind or inside it.

To give them their due, when they realize that they have not seen us for some time they do search for us, combing the house from top to bottom, opening every cupboard and drawer, and even extending their search to the tool shed, the summerhouse and the garage. Consumed by guilt and worry, they know we could be anywhere. Sometimes they find us in a perfectly obvious place, such as in the guest room, quiet inconspicuous humps beneath the duvet. But another time we might be trapped behind a bath panel that has been removed for some repair and then screwed back in place with one of us still dreaming deeply behind it.

It would of course help them to locate us if we responded to their calls. But when we have been shut in a cupboard overnight we are understandably annoyed with them, and don't choose to co-operate. Anyway, it is good for humans to have to make efforts over us, it exercises their brains, as well as reminding them of how important we are to them.

Once, when I was still very small, Meg opened the refrigerator and had quite a shock when I tumbled out of the bottom shelf, half-dead from asphyxiation and hypothermia. But imagine her not having noticed me darting in there a little while before! That was a tragedy narrowly averted—shades of walled-up nuns, mammoths preserved in the Siberian permafrost—I had already imagined myself back in Ancient Egypt, beginning the long slow process of desiccation towards becoming a mummy.

Bill claims we move about invisibly, but of course that is just one of his excuses for human inadequacy. They simply cannot keep up with our rapier sharpness, so perhaps we should not really take offence. Even now there are a dozen places in this small cottage where they never think to check, including the airing cupboard.

When Dido was a small kitten her favourite private place was in a kitchen cupboard that had a carousel in it. It was a time when her dreaming was still largely play. She knew the humans would always look for her there, and that they would get particularly frustrated trying to extricate her, for as fast as they turned the carousel to reach her, she would skip into the next compartment, remaining tantalizingly just out of reach while cans of beans and the like scattered to right and left. She herself kept up a piteous mewing to add to the fun. Dido always has had a streak of pure mischief in her, something I don't share.

But I digress. My intention was not to reminisce about happier days but simply to demonstrate how cats are very much more deeply involved in homemaking than are humans, and how they have put infinitely more into making the place their own. Pleasant though that subject is, we had better return to The Move.

It goes without saying that neither of our humans consulted us cats on the subject of 'pastures new'. We only got to know about it by degrees. Very excited Meg and Bill became. They talked of nothing else. A 'time-warp cottage' they enthused, poring over the estate agent's details—'charming and picturesque, set in a secluded idyllic spot and surrounded by a mature "olde worlde" garden and fine old oak trees.' From which Sedgewick concluded, when we finally told him about it, that our humans had found some gimcrack place tucked away down a rough inconvenient track, and probably in need of considerable repair. But no such negative thoughts seemed to occur to Meg and Bill. All they cared about was that there would be no cars rushing by. Certainly it did not sound the sort of place that the crane could get anywhere near, but nor would there be any more foil trays with exotic titbits flung from car windows to excite poor Sedgewick's fading palate. And clearly no thought had been given as to whether tradesmen's vehicles or the dust cart could get down the narrow rutted track that led to this 'dream cottage'.

As Meg and Bill continued to wax lyrical over details like low ceilings and rough wooden beams, floors on varying levels, original cow-dung plaster walls and bedrooms with windows at floor level, we began to feel a little insecure. None of their enthusiasm rubbed off on us; of course not, we were happy where we were. Sedgewick wondered, dryly, whether the tall clumsy Bill would find it all that much fun hitting his head on those low beams and doorways, and whether Meg would enjoy tripping over the uneven flooring. He also expressed doubts as to whether humans conditioned to central heating would be very happy with an open fire smoking away in a cavernous inglenook.

For a while we succeeded in persuading ourselves that nothing would happen to spoil 'the even tenor of our ways'. We were still in our first carefree year, full of natural bounce and optimism. Comfortably familiar as we were with our house and gardens, we could not believe that all the work we had done to establish our territory would be wasted. No-one surely could expect us to begin all over again?

It was only when we remembered Sedgewick's account of his experience in leaving London that a small cloud of uncertainty began to gather above our heads. As summer advanced and the rumours multiplied, the cloud grew, and with it the first stirrings of resentment began to build in us towards our humans. No cat welcomes change, and we did not see why we should be forced to leave our home against our will.

Sedgewick attempted to comfort us. Apart from his big move to the country, he had also exchanged houses in town on several occasions. He had even once been catnapped. This was when he was still young and very good looking, and a woman unable to resist his black fluffy fur and his pretty triangular face had snatched him up from the street and carried him off in a shopping bag. Sedgewick said she had treated him well enough. But he did not take kindly to being thrust into a shopping bag, nor to being shut up in a strange house. The catnapper kept Sedgewick indoors in order that he would forget his former life and place of domicile—another human fallacy concerning us. Cats never forget anything.

After a month Sedgewick was allowed out and immediately he began to search around for clues as to his whereabouts. It was all entirely new territory to him, he said, but after curling up and pondering the problem for a few hours he began casting about in ever widening circles until suddenly he found himself crossing a familiar street, and in the instant knew exactly where he was. He could recall his whole former territory, including the way back to his rightful home.

This story bears out the scientific theories about cats' use of internal maps which I touched upon earlier—but it was the claim of that being all there was to a cat's intelligence that we objected to.

Sedgewick went back without more ado to Bill and Meg. He said in a way it was a good thing the catnapping had happened because it had extended his territory considerably, as well as making him more wary of strange humans. As an added bonus he said Meg and Bill were even more appreciative of him on his return.

From what our humans said we gathered that the new cottage was only a mile or so away from our present home, so after hearing the story of Sedgewick's catnapping, we thought we too could return to our old haunts if we were not satisfied with the new place. Sedgewick expressed doubts about this, however. He said he had once had a companion called Bootle, another black cat whom Meg and Bill had foisted on him in their mistaken humanitarian notions about cats needing company. Never the brightest of cats, this Bootle had taken it into his head to return to a house that Meg and Bill had just moved from—the new house being no more than a few hundred yards away. (Our humans seem to have made a habit of shifting themselves to nearby houses, perhaps they too have some rudimentary need to remain in touch with familiar territory?)

Anyway, this Bootle apparently was a cat who loved the human race inordinately and unwisely. He took every opportunity of showing his affection by purring deafeningly at them, while kneading away on any part of their anatomy he could get at with his large razor-sharp claws. At the same time he would drool and dribble copiously over the object of his affections.

When the new occupants of Meg and Bill's old home awoke in bed at 5a.m. on their first morning, it was to Bootle's wet ecstatic greetings, and they were not best pleased. Meg was summoned by telephone to remove him. Slow to take a hint, however, Bootle returned and repeated his damp painful salutations every morning at precisely the same time—it was high summer and the sun rose early. Finally Meg, losing patience with the daily retrieval, suggested to the new owners that they should either close the kitchen door to keep Bootle in, or their bedroom door to keep him out or, better still, batten down the cat flap and keep him from entering the house altogether.

Never one to give up without a struggle, shut out of the place he loved, and unable to get in even by hurling himself at the screwed-down cat flap, Bootle mourned. Convinced that he must triumph if only he persevered long enough, he kept the new owners awake for weeks, dolefully yowling beneath their bedroom window. But alas, rejection and hurled missiles were his only reward, and the moral of this tale, said Sedgewick, is don't expect humans to be aware of the honour you confer upon them by choosing to live with them. They are all far denser even than poor Bootle.

Our best hope of evading the trauma of a move and staying put, said Sedgewick, was if the deal fell through. He thought there was a good chance that it might because among this perverse generation of humans who both worship the motor car but at the same time crave peace and quiet, there were many people only too keen to buy inconvenient out-of-the-way cottages far from traffic, like the one Meg and Bill had their hearts set upon. There was a dearth of such property apparently, so when a house situated down a muddy track comes onto the market, crowds descend upon it waving fat cheque books and bits of plastic. Someone might well gazump Bill and Meg said Sedgewick. Indeed our humans had found that someone else was on the point of buying the cottage before they even knew the place existed. It was only because these earlier would-be-buyers were slow about signing the contract that the seller had become impatient, and offered the place to Meg and Bill instead.

But Sedgewick also said not to raise our hopes of staying put too far, for the signs were against us. Our own dear familiar home was clearly on the market. He knew this because of the lawn mower and the vacuum cleaner working overtime. He knew it because of the fresh flowers that were replaced in the vases daily, and the delicious smells of baking bread and fresh-ground coffee that wafted through the house every time strange people appeared. These strangers were escorted through the house and gardens by Meg and Bill dressed in unfamiliarly tidy clothes and holding forth about the many charms of their country cottage.

We spied on these proceedings from hidden corners, trying to think of ways to put off the potential buyers.

There came a sudden lull in the unwelcome

traipsing of strangers through our territory, and we began to breathe more easily. Alas, this was the lull before the storm. We realized our hopes had entirely foundered when large cardboard boxes began to litter the floors of every room. At first they were fun for jumping in and out of, but not for long. Slowly they filled with books. Sixty four boxes full of books! Why cannot humans keep knowledge in their heads as we cats do? Then the china, the ornaments, the clocks! I will refrain from comment on the subject of Bill's obsession with old clocks, sufficient to say their plangent chimes do not aid the process of tuning-in.

By the day of the move summer had departed. Early one grey morning men in brown coats arrived in a huge van into which they began to carry our furniture. Sedgewick, now seventeen, had gone into another decline, and was lying in his gloomiest spot in the garden, no longer able to sustain us. Dido, as was her nature, disassociated herself from the proceedings, and was off hunting across the road—probably imagining herself back in the barbaric glories of Carthage. If ever a cat was well-named, it is my sister Dido. She is a true African Queen—though not one to let herself be got down by a mere male admirer, as did Queen Dido with her Aeneas.

The greatest suffering fell to my lot. I wanted to go right away too but found I could not. It was all too distressing and traumatic.

My lovely comfortable chairs, my soft beautiful carpets; all the trappings of my young life were being bundled up and taken away by strangers. It was a scene like that portrayed on the Assyrian tablets that I had come across in the B.Mus while I was surfing the internet—sad carvings of chained captives being led away into exile, their goods and chattels, following behind them on ox carts—the spoils of war. 'By the waters of Babylon we sat down and wept.' Indeed! And what could a cat like me do at such a time, steeped as I am in the high and classical traditions, but weep?

When my turn came there was no fight left in me. Wrung out with emotion, I was thrust into a horrid hard plastic box called, ironically, a 'Kitty Kabin', and loaded, willy-nilly into a car with my two fellow captives, to be driven into exile like those poor defeated Israelites.

CHAPTER THREE

GREEN FIELDS AND PASTURES NEW

In the natural exuberance of our youth it is possible that some tiny ray of hope still burned in our hearts. Perhaps we had even dared to think that our worst fears would not be realized, and that the experience of moving might yet offer some small saving grace. If so it was in vain. The end of that frightful journey was chaos, confusion and panic. My chairs, my carpets and other much loved household treasures made their welcome reappearance on the shoulders of the same brown-clad men, but now they were disappearing into a strange white-painted cottage that I did not at all like the look of. As I was carried in after them through the low front door, still imprisoned in the hateful Kitty Kabin, I found myself in a dark dingy interior smelling horribly of our arch enemy, dogs. In fact the whole place stank of dogs, big dogs.

Horror of horrors, there were still two of them there, sitting beneath a tree in the garden, at which point I all but fainted. Only when I had recovered a little could I see that these dogs were made of stone. They even looked familiar, as so they should, for they were statues of pharaoh hounds, the oldest representative of all that perfidious race. Later I identified them through the internet as being copies of a sculpture in the Victoria and Albert Museum in London. They had been purchased, I learnt from Meg, to mark the grave of one of the pharaoh hounds which had lived in this cottage. Much as I loathe all dogs, this link with the happier lives of our ancestors in Ancient Egypt had a steadying effect upon me, and I was able to rally Dido to take a renewed interest in life.

Bill had decided we should be shut in the house until we had got used to the place. But the upstairs windows were open, and being indeed conveniently set at floor level, it was no big deal to jump out of them once we had been released from the Kitty Kabins.

The first duty was a quick reconnoitre, so as

to know the worst. This at least confirmed that no live dogs remained. In fact there was nothing at all threatening inside the high chainlink fence which surrounded the entire garden so reassuringly. Deep gouging on trees and doors and wooden posts showed where the newly-vanished hounds had made many previous bids for freedom. Pharaoh hounds, as the departed dogs undoubtedly were, are bred to course tirelessly after game all day long through the hot desert sands. They must have loathed their lives confined in a small English garden. Ruthless killers as they are, it was as well for us that only their stone replicas remained.

By the way, anyone interested in these archaic-looking hounds, and unable to go to the V and A to see the statue of them, can get a good idea of what they look like from studying the jackal-headed Egyptian god. Pharaoh hounds look just like the enormous-eared Anubis—not I might say, my favourite deity of the Egyptian pantheon.

But back to our recce.

After a short while we realized we could smell another dog close by. Then we saw it, and once again my heart almost stopped. As for Dido, her eyes grew so round and wide they looked like saucers. There was no doubting that it was a dog, although it was the size of a donkey, and the bark it gave when it saw us was worse even than the noise of the great tractors roaring up the hill. Thanks be to Great Sahkmet, friend and protector of our race, that this monster was outside the high perimeter fence. Had it been on the same side as us, I think we might have remained in a state of paralysis, and fallen victim to its slavering jaws, so great was the shock caused by its appearance.

This Great Dane, (for so we subsequently discovered it to be) was a fixture of the place. He could never become a friend of ours, of course, but we were neighbours and had therefore to preserve some semblance of cordiality. We knew that the creature's brain was in no way in keeping with his vast size, and that we were easily able to outwit him. Even so, we preferred to put our faith in stout fencing. 'Good fences make good neighbours' the saying goes, and so it proved with this overgrown canine. His fence kept him in, and we never seriously fell out.

This last point had added significance, for we soon learnt that the strong high chain-link fence which had kept the pharaoh hounds in and, more importantly, kept potential attackers out, was to come down. This lion fence, as Bill and Meg called it, was not to their liking. You could be excused for thinking that even humans would have realized the worth of such a splendid security barrier. You might also assume that the first priority was to concentrate on making the living quarters comfortable for their cats. But ignoring everyone else's needs, Meg and Bill said they had no intention of living inside Fort Knox for a minute longer than they needed. Even before they moved in they had arranged for a contractor to replace the admirable steel palisade with a low wooden stock fence.

Disturbingly wide views immediately opened up all around, and the house and garden lay exposed to assault on all sides. The new low fence had the added insult of being trenched into the ground to keep rabbits out. Out of the garden, mark you, a valuable wholesome food source turned away from where we could have pounced upon it with ease as it nibbled at the lettuces.

It was forestry next. A double row of thirty cupressus leylandii trees, planted as a hedge along one side of the garden, in order to break the force of the prevailing south-westerly winds had, apparently, been 'let go' by the previous occupants, and were now dark towering giants of sixty and seventy feet. We thought they were doing a splendid job of shielding the garden, as well as providing a lovely dark dry mysterious place where we could lurk in wait for birds and rodents. But once again our humans thought they knew best. The leylandii shut out all the best views of the valley, they said, and were also robbing other trees in the garden of light and space. They had to go.

So while we camped disconsolately among shrouded furniture stacked in the dust and soot and cobwebs of decades, the chainsaws shrilled horribly, and a giant machine of unspeakable and earth-shattering virulence scrunched up the branches, and vomited them out in great gushing mounds of smashed fragments all over the pathway that led down to the fields.

The garden, when we first saw it, was a world away from the smooth well-tended lawns from which we had been so peremptorily torn. It was a rough, weed-infested wilderness, full of deep holes and hollows where the pharaoh hounds had dug pits and attempted to uproot trees, in their frustration and desire to escape. They had even ring-barked many of the trees, including a huge willow that overhung the pond, or what would have been a pond if the same dogs had not torn apart the stones of the lining, so that instead of water it held nothing but a tangle of mud, weeds and rocks.

Unattractive this new garden had certainly looked, but under Meg's and Bill's onslaughts it quickly grew far worse. Electricity cables that had formerly been draped along the top of the chain link fence, from where they had made long interesting loops across to greenhouses, to various sheds, to a garage and to a small summerhouse, now disappeared into trenches dug for them across the lawn. These jagged furrows, together with the stumps of the leylandii and the mounds of earth left from enlarging the foundations of the garage, made of the garden a muddy obstacle course rather than a pleasance fit for cats. We mourned silently for the comfortable 'des res' we had left.

Strange contrasts in this wrecked and blighted scene were the two beautiful pharaoh hound statues and a very large and elegant wrought iron weathervane taken from the roof of some eighteenth-century civic structure and set down in the centre of the blighted lawns, as bizarrely misplaced as the lamp-post in Narnia. The presence of these ornaments, weathervane and dogs, became for us an important symbol, especially so for me. They proclaimed a belief in the existence of better things, of a more cultured, ordered and expansive lifestyle. I saw them as offering hope for a more favourable future. On fine days when there were no rough workmen about I took to sitting on the plinth of the weathervane, my back protected by its strong column, as I gazed out along the cardinal compass points. For what seemed a very long time it was my one fixed point of reference in a turbulent and troubled world.

While I think of it, I cannot remember if I have mentioned the astonishing fact that Meg was not with us for The Move? Well, she was not. About a week before the fateful day she departed to the other side of the world, on what she called 'a whistle-stop lecture tour' for some literary festival in New Zealand.

What can one say about such dereliction of duty? What sort of human is it who could desert her responsibilities in this way, and at such a time? Remember, it is young cats at a particularly vulnerable stage of their development who were being put in jeopardy, not to mention the poor aged Sedgewick who was by now thinking about shaking out his celestial robes.

Without the assistance of Meg, Bill had to manage the whole move on his own—if manage is the right word. Muddle through would be a distinct understatement for describing the chaos that ensued.

When Meg showed up four weeks later, it was to a cottage that had become little more than a furniture repository, and a badly managed repository at that. Neither human had considered how little furniture can be piled up beneath the beams of low-ceilinged rooms, nor how to work around such daunting obstacles.

If Bill was responsible for creating the original chaos, Meg's return saw the confusion doubled and redoubled. While the demolition work went into full gear in the garden, a similar scene of destruction began inside. Nothing could be put in order, it appeared, until further disorder was created, and endless alterations made. Floors were dug up and relaid, bedroom ceilings raised, windows replaced, central heating installed, and walls and ceilings re-plastered throughout. There was nowhere that did not require extensive renovation and decorating. While the whole place was turned into one extended building site, three cats and two humans had to do their best to survive in it.

Dust and dirt! Dirt and dust! I shudder even now at the memory of it. I must have swallowed a sack of plaster, and all of it painstakingly cleaned from my fur. All day long men dug and shovelled, hammered, sawed and mixed cement and plaster. Or else they sat around drinking tea, while they waited for the lorries which brought further quantities of floor tiles, wall tiles, plasterboard, wallpaper, paint, window frames and doors, and many other things I did not even recognise, but all of which added to the general mess and confusion. Some of the lorries got stuck along the track, and valuable time was lost digging them out.

Attempting to escape the worse of the turmoil by hiding among the piled-up furniture, I several times experienced the trauma of stacks of chairs and mattresses collapsing around me. My nerves were shot to pieces.

The only immoveable object in all this desolation was in the kitchen, in the form of a stove called Aga, which stayed blissfully warm all the time, night and day. Our catflap was in the door of the kitchen, so that we cats could sleep at nights alongside the life-preserving warmth, and I am convinced that it was only this amiable stove, together with the Victorian weathervane in the ruined garden, which saved me from despair.

The worst time, the very nadir of our young lives, came in the middle of a cold wind-plagued November, when one perfectly sound outside wall in the kitchen was knocked down and replaced with plastic sheets. This was because the humans fancied a larger room with wider views of the garden. Why they could not go outside to enjoy their views, as we do, is just one further instance of human perversity.

A hole was cut into the bottom of the plastic sheet so that we could still go in and out, and through this the wind blew with unrelenting ferocity. I am amazed we survived it at all.

Only Sedgewick, daily declining a little further, appeared undisturbed by the horrors of The Move. He was by now as thin as a wraith, although he continued to eat well and had no pain. He was simply fading away from old age, and Meg and Bill could do little for him other than to make sure he could get in and out to the garden when he wanted and that he had his comfortable warm place beside the stove. There he stayed, not moving much, his deafness protecting him from the worst of the noise and turmoil. And it was here at nights, after the workmen had departed and the humans were in bed, that Sedgewick continued to unfold his store of knowledge, passing on to us young cats all that he knew of the world and of the place of the feline race within it. We listened with due reverence and attention realizing that he could not postpone his departure for very much longer. These were blessed periods of peace for us in the hectic business of getting the cottage fit for habitation.

And, as Sedgewick daily assured us, no horror endures for ever. By Christmas, and only just before the first snow fell, the worst was over. A little order began to creep into our lives again. Another month or two and we would be thoroughly civilized, with fresh paint on all the walls, carpets on the floors, furniture properly arranged, and the humans once more sitting at the dining table for their meals.

Only one of us was not there to enjoy it. On New Year's Day, from his cushion beside the Aga, our dear friend and mentor, Sedgewick, set out on his long celestial journey. We did not watch as our humans buried the weightless shell at the bottom of the garden overlooking the meadows and the river. We curled up in our best places and willed ourselves to dream him onwards through the highways of the stars.

CHAPTER FOUR

THE MOVE ACCORDING TO DIDO

Hallo, a change of storyteller. I am to have a proper turn on the writing machine now, instead of just putting in the odd bits. I am Dido, usually called Diddy or Diddypuss, sometimes even Did. I am the one who looks like the kitten in Hogarth's painting of the Graham children. If you have seen this very lovely picture in the National Gallery in London you will know that I am a young bright-eyed tabby cat with big paws, claws usually half way out in eager anticipation.

Altogether the born mouser.

My sister Sappho says it is a very special privilege to have tabby markings because that is what the Ancient Egyptian cats had, and everyone knows that they were the ancestors of all modern cats. Being tabbies means that we are in the direct line, and therefore the most special cats in the world. Privileges aside, I do realize how fortunate I am in being tabby all over. It provides the most perfect camouflage for slipping unnoticed along the hedgerows and through the copses. Poor old Sapphy's dazzling white bits (of which she is so proud) show up like warning beacons.

Hunting is what I like best so Nimrod, Orion, or even Diana would have been better names for me than Dido. To tell the truth, I don't have much time for my namesake. I just can't see the sense in getting all worked up over some bloke who chooses to push off in a boat (and to Italy of all places) rather than staying put in Carthage where he could have married the queen and enjoyed all the hunting he wanted. But since sailing off is what Aeneas chose to do, well Good Luck to him I say. I wouldn't have wanted him hunting alongside me with half his mind on other things—far too risky. Anyway, to go and kill oneself for love is something no cat would ever do, it's against nature. And I wouldn't want to have a soppy song called Dido's Lament written about me either, even though Sapphy says it is one of the greatest female arias of all time.

I hadn't really meant to go on about Dido and Aeneas. I usually leave that sort of thing to Sappho who is more up in the classics than I am. My learned, romantic and often intensely irritating sister and housemate is altogether different from me. Very serious is Sappho and, at the same time, over-sensitive and easily offended. She says I spend far too much of my time playing when I should be engaged in more serious feline matters. It is time I grew up she says. But I tell her I am making the most of being young, and that it will be time enough to settle down when I am middle-aged.

Sapphy sometimes pretends she would be better off without me, but I am not fooled. 'Cats don't need company,' she intones in that annoying superior way she has. I think she says it because she misses bossing me about like she did when we were small kittens. Sappho likes to be in charge. It is a pity she ever had the operation for I am sure she would have enjoyed being a mother cat.

Of course we don't do everything together anymore like we used to; now we are fully-grown we need our own space. Sharing a territory requires compromise and the right attitude, and mostly we are very civilized about this. Only very occasionally do we spit at each other, or unsheathe our deadly claws. Even at the most stressful moments I try to remember my place as younger sister, and in everything, apart from hunting, I usually give way to big sister Sappho.

After The Move, Sapphy became more of an indoor cat while I still choose to spend most of my time outside. I think she gets a bit jealous sometimes when she sees all the mice I catch. She has grown a bit too fat for active stalking, but I let her come hunting with me sometimes, making sure, of course, that she keeps her tell-tale white bits well hidden in the undergrowth. All in all, we remain very fond of each other and still touch noses in passing. The only time I am likely to growl a warning nowadays (I do assure you cats can growl) is when Sappho muscles in on my walks in the garden with Meg and Bill. I chase her away then because this is my time with my humans, and I want all their attention. They do not have that much to spare.

It is strange about cats and humans; we have such different natures, and yet we get on so well together. Sapphy says humans are more dependent on us than we are on them. She says it is our duty to be with them, and bring them to what she calls a proper appreciation of the important things of life. She calls this 'the cats' burden'. But I am not sure that she has got it quite right. Hunter though I am and very independent, I would feel a bit lost without my humans to come home to. I know they have forgotten how to communicate with other creatures and all that. But sometimes in the evenings, in front of a log fire, while Meg and Bill play music or read a book or watch television, it feels to me almost as if we were one family. Even Sappho forgets her dignity then. She lies on her back on the hearthrug, paws in the air, exposing her fat white stomach to the cheerful glow. Sapphy loves the fire so much she sometimes has to be moved back from it before she singes her whiskers.

I am not a fire worshipper myself, my coat is too thick. I like the cheerful leaping flames, but at a distance. On family evenings I usually squeeze into the high-backed wing chair with Meg. This chair is really one of my own special places but Meg hasn't realized this yet; she is slow in such matters, and often sits in places I have already reserved. There isn't really enough room in the cosy draught-proof armchair for both of us, but being hard and fit means I can wriggle in and make Meg squeeze up to one side so that I can lay at full stretch with my paws hanging relaxed over the edge. With Meg propping me up snugly on one side and the chair arm on the other, I am even more comfortable than when I have the whole chair to myself.

Interruption: Sappho says I have to stop writing all this stuff about fires and chairs and things because this chapter is supposed to be about how I saw The Move. She says I have had more than enough time for the introduction, and either I get on to the subject and stick to it, or I will have to get off the writing machine and let her take over. So, more cosy chat about fires, chairs and comfort and things later on. First 'The Move'.

Well, the truth is that secretly, I was glad to be taken away. The road at the other place had become really scary. It is hard to explain exactly, but there was something about that road that challenged me, even though I knew it spelt terrible danger. It was not even a pleasant place. I hated the stink of it; hated the hot sticky grip of the asphalt and the searing breath-stopping blasts of exhaust gasses from the swift rushing cars that seemed to be out to get me. The deafening thunder of the huge juggernauts spelt pure terror. Yet somehow the road excited me with a sort of sick fascination, so that I found myself dashing to and fro across it as much as a dozen times a day, missing the wheels of vehicles by inches. It had become a drug.

Dear old Sedgewick often sat in the cottage garden watching my performance with the traffic, and he took me aside one day to tell me that in London cats had a name for what I was doing—Russian Roulette, he said they called it; and he also said that when cats got hooked on that game they did not last long.

Being a London cat, born and bred, Sedgewick knew a great deal about roads and traffic and their effect upon certain felines. His own house mate, the cat called Bootle, had also fallen prey to the thrill of Russian Roulette. Sedgewick told me of how Bootle had taken to dicing with death on a busy road near their London home, and had quickly exhausted eight of his free lives in spectacular near-misses. He spent his ninth, and what should have been his final innings, in a headlong collision with a car. The injuries he sustained were frightful, said Sedgewick. They included a broken jaw, the loss of several teeth, a tail much reduced in length, and the destruction of enough brain cells to render him even thicker than he had previously been.

Sedgewick made me realize that it could be only a matter of time before I too suffered a similar fate on our hairpinned killer of a road. I began to have nightmares about it—maimed, blinded, crippled, brain damaged—a cabbage cat! All night long I would toss and turn, keeping Sapphy awake. She got thoroughly fed up with me, and began sleeping apart, which made me even more miserable. Even so I was still unable to resist the lure of that wild exhilarating death-defying dash across the dreaded tarmac.

Another interruption: Sapphy is now asking whether I am telling Bootle's story or just boasting about being silly on the road? Whichever it is, she says, it has nothing at all to do with The Move. I must say this story telling is not nearly as easy as I thought it would be. It is jolly difficult to get everything down in the right place. But now I have started on it, I think I must finish Bootle's story before we go on about our own affairs. Otherwise I might forget to put it in, and I am sure that the readers are as curious as I was to know what happened to him.

Had the foolhardy Bootle not been blessed with a super-feline constitution, as well as owning humans who were prepared to pay to have him mended, said Sedgewick, that ninth encounter would have been the end of him. As it was, it cost Bill and Meg a packet to get him put right, and Bootle had to stay at the vets for weeks. He was in a lot of pain, with his jaw wired up and being fed through tubes. But it ended all right because he lived on happily for another five years. He avoided the road ever afterwards, shuddering a bit whenever he found himself near it. He would give it a look of deep reproach, said Sedgewick, as though to say he hadn't forgiven it for hurting him so badly.

Bootle had always been a simple soul, and now he spent most of his time trying to join in the games of the younger children in the square. They were rather embarrassed by his persistence and by his dribbling over them—the dribbling was worse than before because of the lost teeth. Sometimes the children complained to Meg or Bill, saying Bootle wouldn't leave them alone and was spoiling their games, but being nice children they learnt to ignore his less pleasant features, and usually just let him trail around after them.

Then, at the age of twelve, Bootle suffered a sudden and severe onslaught of galloping senility, a condition rare in cats, and probably the result of his head injury, together with the anaesthetics used in the mending of him. He took to pacing round endlessly in ever tighter circles, looking puzzled and distressed. Clearly the time had come for him to move on.

Sedgewick says cats know when it is time for them to set out on the long celestial journey, but that in his confused state, poor Bootle was unable to make his exit for himself. Meg and Bill had to take him to the vets to start him on his way, which, I am told, is a very hard thing for humans to have to do.

Right, that's all finished now about Bootle. Back to The Move.

Without doubt, it was only The Move that saved me from a fate like Bootle's. But, even allowing for this reprieve, I do have to agree with Sappho that when it came, The Move (we always think of it in capital letters) was a bit of a shock. Well, all right then Sapphy, it was much worse than that; it was truly awful. Picture, if you can, the panic we felt at being thrust suddenly into a small confining basket; the constraint, the confusion, the slamming of doors, the terrifying car ride. All the dreadful noises and strange alarming scents were made immeasurably worse by the horrible wailing cries of terror which were wrung from our own throats, but which seemed to come from somewhere else altogether, somewhere far outside our control.

When this ghastly journey was finally over there was little feeling of relief because we found ourselves in terrifying new surroundings to which we had no chart, no key. We were off the edge of the known world—*Terra Incognita*, a 'Here be Dragons' country.

As Sapphy has already told you, there was a strange white cottage which reeked of dogs. Then we saw the two dogs in the garden sitting alert and poised, ready to pounce on us. Being in the state we were, it was a moment or two before we realized that these dogs were only stone ones. But no sooner had we taken in this comforting fact, than we saw snuffling towards us a truly monstrous and unmistakeably live dog, a terrifying apparition as big as a small horse. This nightmare of a creature had great ropes of saliva hanging from its reeking jaws in anticipation of the unexpected double titbit of plump little cats.

Later we came to know that this overgrown canine was called a Great Dane and was by no means the awful threat he appeared. In fact he was really rather pathetic, a result of human interference with dogs' natural breeding patterns. Butcher, as he was called, suffered from all sorts of ailments—weak heart, painful joints and so on, all caused, he explained, by generations of being bred for size at the expense of all a dog's other natural attributes. To cap it all, the poor thing had only a very short life expectancy. But then, considering all that was wrong with him, this was probably a good thing.

Of course this information about Great Danes came later. When we first set eyes on Butcher he appeared to us as the embodiment of all the demons we had ever read about. Had there not been a stout fence to foil his advance, it would have been curtains for us, because we were rivetted to the spot, mesmerized by terror, and had Butcher's huge but weak jaws failed to crush the life from us, we would doubtless have died of fright.

Writing this brings back a time that is best forgotten. Indeed I had forgotten it until forced to recall it by Sappho. Because you see, once the initial shock of the arrival had passed, and I started to learn my new territory, I began to see what had attracted Meg and Bill to make the move to this new place. They had, I realized, got it right.

For one thing, the cottage was in real countryside, right out of the way. There was no road running past it, only a track, and no close neighbours either. Indeed, we could not see another house from the cottage, not in the summer anyway. There were fields all around the garden, with hedgerows and lots of trees, so the hunting was bound to be good. And there was no sodium glare to spoil the night sky. I could stalk game like my forebears, by starshine and moonlight, as though the world was still young, and street lighting and motor cars had not been invented.

Being more of a house cat, Sappho suffered far more from The Move than I did. While I explored the new surroundings, she stayed close to the household effects. Still in deepest mourning for her orderly life in the picture book cottage from which she had so recently been wrenched, Sappho would cower under upturned armchairs or wriggle beneath rugs where she imagined she was invisible. Startled by plumbers, electricians and painters, she would leap onto upended mattresses which folded under the onslaught, and once precipitated her down the stairwell. It was definitely not a happy time for my poor sister.

Both house and gardens were a horrid mess, that I could not deny. With winter coming on fast, I hoped our people would hurry up and get it all warm and catworthy. Until they did I stayed out of the way, catching so many nice fat mice in the richly populated hedgerows that I could afford to comfort my sister with a few of them. Sappho's appetite is never noticeably diminished by suffering.

To be honest, I didn't have as much sympathy with Sapphy's misery as I might have done. I thought there should be more important things in a cat's life than an elegant house and velvet lawns, and I reminded her of the verse in Matthew which she had been fond of quoting to me. It was 'Lay not up for yourself treasures upon earth . . .' But I don't think I was being quite fair because if the house is where your heart is what can a cat do? And anyway, who was I to criticize? I too was laying up earthly treasures for myself, they just happened to be different ones from Sapphy's.

For I was falling in love with my new territory. As I said, Meg and Bill had got it right, and like them, I never once felt the least craving for my former haunts, even while Fairfield was at its most squalid and least comfortable. As far as I was concerned, it had far more going for it than the 'des res' we had recently left. I'll try and describe the world of Fairfield for you so that you can see what I mean.

To reach the cottage you leave a quiet narrow winding country lane by an even narrower track that has grass down the middle of it and hedgerows on either side, hedgerows that are stuffed full with wildlife and as good as a larder. The humans loved this lane too, but for different reasons; they prefer flowers and birds to mice. Sedgewick had guessed rightly that the dustbin truck couldn't get down this track, but Meg and Bill didn't mind that they had to take their plastic rubbish sacks down in the wheelbarrow every Monday morning; it was an opportunity for an early walk. At first, they were worried when they saw me trailing after them, for they hadn't realized I had given up Russian Roulette. (Dicing with death would hardly have been much of a thrill on that backwater country lane with only one or two cars an hour to choose from, anyway.) I just went along on the rubbish run with Meg and Bill for the company, and sometimes I rode back in the empty wheelbarrow. Another track goes down the side of the cottage, a cool, dim, secret way, sloping gently down to where a spring wells up into a little round pond surrounded by purple flags. This was once the water supply for the cottage before indoor taps were invented. Beyond the pond, around a bend, the sunken green way continues, dropping down below the level of the garden and the fields which flank it on either side.

Bill says that this track once led down to a jetty on the river, where coal and other goods for the hamlet folk were unloaded from barges. But now it goes nowhere at all, ending at the gate leading to the water meadows. I only venture into the open spaces of these fields when I am out walking with my humans, because if I am there alone the sheep bunch up and loom over me and I feel threatened. But the green lane itself was always my most special place. I loved it from the beginning, as I am sure you would too. The best thing about it is the closely-planted tall trees that line its entire length. Gnarled old oak and ash trees for the most part, some of them are burdened with towering swathes of ivy. Their branches spread out mightily, meeting overhead with the thorn trees and field maples growing on the edge of the cottage garden, so that in full summer the track becomes a green tunnel.

A deep ditch in front of the trees drains the surrounding fields, but is dry for most of the year and lined with ferns and wild flowers. Beyond the trees is a thirty-acre field, visible only in winter, when the branches are black tracery against the red western sky. Thick twisted roots break surface in the ditch's banks, creating many exciting hollow places, home to colonies of mice, voles, squirrels and shrews. Here I hunt alone by day, and with the owls, stoats, weasels, foxes and badgers by night. And still there remains plenty for us all.

Sappho also loves the green lane, and spent a lot of her time monitoring what is going on among the treetops. There being windows on three sides of our kitchen, Sapphy gets most of her exercise by leaping from window sill to window sill, following the movements of squirrels and birds, chittering with excitement, especially when one particular squirrel decides to tease her by playing easy to catch.

Soon after our arrival, I was enticed into pursuing this annoying squirrel, and I got myself stuck very high up in one of the oaks, and Bill went round the neighbourhood trying, without success, to borrow a long ladder to rescue me. Sappho, who can never bear to see her sister in distress, heard my cries and decided to rescue me herself. When Sapphy does go out she amazes me by her agility in the trees: I have to admit she is the better climber. But on this occasion, when the humans returned ladderless and shone their torch up into the tree, the beam picked out not one but two young cats clinging to a narrow branch. Rather than getting me down, I had infected Sappho with my terror, and now we were both marooned on the high swaying perch, mewing piteously.

Meg called for help from the fire brigade. A sensible girl answered the call and told the distraught Meg that most cats stuck in trees will come down safely of their own accord when they get really hungry. If we were still up there in twenty-four hours' time, she promised to send a rescue team. It was hard for Meg and Bill to eat their supper that night and to go to bed, all within sight and sound of two hungry cats still firmly treed and mewing pitifully.

The fire brigade girl was right of course. Hunger did finally lend us the necessary courage to return to *terra firma*. The problem we cats have with climbing downwards is that we prefer to proceed head first, both going up and coming down. Squirrels can easily scamper head first down a bare tree trunk. Alas we are not built like squirrels, and when branches are too far apart for us to spring from one to the next, we have to reverse and come down tail first, gripping the trunk with our claws, rather like koala bears. Not all cats can manage this backwards slither. We can, but it doesn't feel natural, and even after all our practice it still requires great courage to push our tails over the edge of a branch and launch ourselves blindly downwards from a high perch.

It was 4 a.m. before we were able to make the move. Cold, hungry but triumphant, we were pleased to see that our humans had not closed their bedroom door as they usually do. We had no hesitation at all about jumping on the bed to inform them that we were back and 'where was our dinner?' To give them their due, they seemed very glad to see us, though usually they are cross if we manage to get into their room and wake them up in the night.

Meg and Bill are also fond of trees, although they don't seem often to want to climb them. A view of treetops fills the bathroom window, and I've seen both Meg and Bill lying up to their necks in bubbly hot water watching the teeming birdlife in the upper branches. I sometimes sit on the edge of the bath to keep them company, and I work out tactics for sneaking up on those birds. But a bath makes a perilous perch, and as soon as washing begins I scamper off fast so as not to get my fur splashed.

Oh dear I see another lecture coming up!

My sister Sappho says lyrical descriptions of the countryside, and baths and such like have nothing at all to do with The Move. All that could have come in a later chapter, she says. First we have to write about getting the cottage straight, because there were not any window sills to sit upon, nor a bath to soak in until everything had been got right and put in order.

As far as I am concerned Sappho has already written enough about all that boring stuff. I decided the cottage was already straight, and I had better things to write about. It is really still my turn on the writing machine, but I have had enough of being interrupted and, to tell the truth, my paws do feel a bit sore with all this tapping. Sappho can take over if she wants to.

We would return to Sappho and sanity in order to round off the subject of The Move, except that we seem to have used up all our time on the machine for today. Any clearing up of loose ends will just have to wait now for the next chapter.

CHAPTER FIVE

NEIGHBOURHOOD HOSTILITIES

Dido's dashing style and wealth of *non sequiturs* has put the subject of The Move right out of my head. I think we had better just forget about tying up any loose ends, and get on with the next phase of our life in Fairfield.

There was barely time to bask in the restored domestic comfort of the cottage before fresh horrors surfaced in the shape of neighbourhood hostility. Either from fear or from a not quite vanished respect for age, the cats of the hamlet had waited until Sedgewick had departed on his celestial voyage before launching their attack. By now it was early spring, a time when territorial matters loom large among the birds and animals of the fields and woodlands. Cats, with their less hide-bound approach to mating, are not usually so affected by the seasons. Not so the Fairfield cats. They responded to Spring by becoming noticeably meaner and more aggressive.

That rancour existed towards us in our new home was a fact we had already accepted. Whispers from the proprietorial inhabitants of the place had reached us from the first. 'Who did we think we were, "incumden felines", muscling in on the territory of decent country cats?' "Townee rubbish" most like, and certainly up to no good.'

Sedgewick had tried to explain to us what lay behind this sour dislike. Although himself a town cat born and bred, he knew more than we did about the suspicious natures of rural animals. Actually Sedgewick knew a great deal about most things, having had more opportunities for modern study than the average cat. He was particularly sound on sociology, having once attended an extramural course at the prestigious London School of Economics. Cats living in university towns experience little difficulty in acquiring higher education. Few humans will remark their presence around the halls of learning as being anything unusual. As long as a cat maintains a modest but purposeful demeanour, he is usually assumed to belong to the place, and is able to come and go as he pleases. Curled up on benches in lecture halls or ensconced beneath chairs during tutorials, with a listening ear and a retentive memory, many a cat has acquired the equivalent of a first-class honours degree. In just such a way, by the exercise of his native talents, Sedgewick had procured for himself a broad and liberal education.

'Town air makes free,' Sedgewick was fond of quoting in support of his theory that city life has a refining influence upon those cats sensitive enough to benefit from the rich cultural and educational opportunities to be found there. He also claimed that having to live in close proximity with others in the confined spaces of a town made for greater tolerance and social awareness, as well as for better manners.

Interruption from Dido: I thought that what Sedgewick meant was that in town you had either to get on together or else fight to the death?

That is the negative way of looking at it of course Dido, but I suppose it comes to the same thing in the end. Shall we get on?

The many snippets Sedgewick knew by heart from Adam Smith and from Thomas Paine's *The Rights of Man* revealed our old friend as rather dangerously left of centre in his politics—not at all the type to appeal to true-blue rural England. 'But we are country cats,' Dido and I had protested. 'We were born and weaned within hearing of these same village church bells. We belong here.'

'That has nothing to do with it,' retorted Sedgewick. 'You'll find that out here in the sticks you are only as good as the humans you live with, and you will be tarred with the same brush as them. There is no such thing as equality in the country. You will be "townee's cats", "too clever by half", and "weird" into the bargain.'

'You won't stand a chance of cordial relations with the average cat around here,' continued Sedgewick inexorably. 'Just take a long cool look at your humans. Nothing to do with whether you like them or not, with whether they are kind and considerate. Even if they were absolute rotters the only thing that matters here in rural England is do they fit? And the answer must be plain even to you naive little purrers; they do not. Just look at

70

their general appearance, not a waxed Barbour jacket or a pair of green hunter wellies between them. And as for the vehicles they go about in, you especially, Dido, have surely seen enough passing traffic to realize that a Range Ranger, a Mercedes, or even a Volvo is light years away from a Citroen 2 c.v.! It is true that Bill also owns a BMW, but as that is a motor bike it weights the scales even further against them. And what are they usually seen out and about on? Precisely. They wander openly around the countryside on push-bikes! Have I made my point?'

'Appearance and conformity, that is what counts in the country. Poverty is perfectly acceptable, for it makes those with more wealth feel superior. But to have money and not to spend it on cultivating the correct image is not alright. It is eccentric, and eccentricity arouses suspicion; folk don't know where they are with the unconventional. "If we ain't come across it before it must be bad," is a prime country maxim, the other side of which is "Look there's a stranger, lets 'eave half a brick at him."

'An even greater mistake made by our humans is their buying that ten-acre field. For incumdens to buy land is a cheek; for eccentric incumdens to buy land is outrageous, deeply suspicious too, especially if they don't want to make money out of it. You ask how this concerns you? Deep in rural England, my stripey young hopefuls, the saying goes "Like owners, like animals." Face the facts you dear, plump little innocents. Either you pack your knapsacks now and try to charm your way into a more conforming household, or you will just have to toughen up and learn to become self-sufficient misfits, like Bill and Meg.'

By small signs—warning scents left around our perimeter fencing—spiteful midnight caterwauling, the twitch of a vanishing tail, the sounds of sudden departure in the undergrowth—we came to realize that Sedgewick had been right. We could expect trouble.

It came one dark and windy night, when Dido and I were out playing, pretending we were still carefree kittens chasing a few of last year's dry scurrying leaves about the garden. Caught offguard, and too far from the house to bolt for the cat flap, we could only turn and face our assailants.

We hope we gave a good account of ourselves in spite of our lack of practice in fighting. The damage we sustained, apart from the shock and indignity, was an honourable bite in a foreleg for me, and one in a rear leg for poor Dido.

Another digression:

'Yes Dido, I know you were not running away, and that one particularly malicious cat got behind you while you were face to face with another huge brute. But it still remains the fact that your wound was in a rear leg, while mine was to the front. All right? You don't have to feel bad about it Diddy. It doesn't mean you are a coward. Some cats are just quicker than others, that's all.'

We thought it very bad form that we should be attacked on our own territory, and it must convey something of the low nature of our assailants that both wounds turned septic and required several traumatic visits to the vet and the horrid business of having antibiotic pills thrust down our throats every morning. First round to the enemy.

Wrapped in our own problems we had not realized that Meg and Bill were also being savaged, only rather more subtly; at least no-one actually bit them. In their case the first attack was a sudden descent upon the cottage by a council official. It happened when the house was still in a state of chaos, with workmen everywhere. Meg was hard at work, tapping away on the writing machine in a cleared space at the end of the garage, wrapped against the cold in several rugs and a balaclava helmet. With the deadline for delivery of her latest manuscript fast approaching, she was aware only of the screen

73

in front of her.

It was fortunate that Bill saw the inspector first—authors are not at their best when disturbed in the throes of their creative wrestlings—as my sister and I can now fully appreciate. But in any case, Bill is usually of a more even temperament than is Meg, and does not immediately think that any setback is 'The End'.

The council official appeared nervous and somewhat embarrassed as though expecting trouble. He seemed somewhat taken aback by Bill's quiet manner and polite diplomacy, as though he was more used to abuse and defiance.

'There have been complaints,' he said. 'Running a business from domestic premises is not allowed; nor is the building of huge extensions and putting up garages without permission, especially in an area of outstanding natural beauty. Our informant was very worried about all the comings and goings there would be, ruining the peaceful nature of the area.'

'If you call writing books a business then we plead guilty,' said a mystified Bill, 'though it hasn't so far resulted in many comings and goings. My wife, unfortunately for our bank balance, has not yet become the subject of a "literary trail". As for the "huge extension", can you possibly mean that little bit in the patio that has been added to the kitchen? We were told it was too small to require planning permission. And the garage is merely a replacement for an older one on the same site which was falling down. We have replaced it with this one which is only very slightly larger and considerably nicer in appearance. Who on earth has been saying such silly things about us?'

'I am not at liberty to tell you that, sir,' replied the inspector, relaxing a little. 'Most informants choose to remain anonymous. The council receives hundreds of complaints yearly, and at least three quarters of them turn out to be malicious. But we, of course, are obliged to investigate them all.'

Once the small extension to the kitchen had been measured and found to be within permitted limits, and the hundred identical cardboard boxes in the garage had been proved to hold nothing more commercial than a well-thumbed library of books awaiting their shelves, the inspector departed with due apologies, putting his morning's work down to clearing up yet one more case of neighbourly ill-will.

Dido and I could hear the neighbourhood cats spitting with rage at the outcome of this visit. The official's car had been spotted, and they had been lurking under nearby hedgerows hoping to witness our humans' come-uppance.

For Meg and Bill the incident left a nasty taste, as do all such hostile acts, especially the anonymous kind. There were only a half dozen households in the vicinity, and since they had all evinced the same sour unfriendliness towards our humans it could have been any or all of them who had made the calls to the council. Humans are less adaptable than cats, and far less able to cope with dislike and hostility from their own kind. We felt quite sorry for them.

But what saddened Dido and me most was that members of the noble race of cats should have sunk so low as to have abandoned their hereditary and sacred task of bringing benign influences to bear upon the humans with whom they lived. Clearly their households stood in urgent need of such influence, but in Fairfield it seemed that it was the cats who were being perversely influenced by their humans. At least four thousand years have passed since our ancestors assumed their high ethical position in the Middle Kingdom of Ancient Egypt, but to judge from these furry bundles of crabby spite you would not have known they had sprung from the same illustrious race. Indeed you could have been forgiven for assuming they were descendants of the most brutish of beasts, of dogs even.

Sedgewick had often tried to talk to us about the moral danger of cats forgetting who and what they are. But sheltered innocents as we then were, we had not followed his argument. Nor had we yet fully understood the nature of the cats' sacred role. We knew we were very special of course. The knowledge that cats are naturally superior is innate; even foundling kittens have it. And all other creatures, including humans, should be able to deduce our high degree from our general demeanour. But as Sedgewick was at pains to explain, behaviour is only the outward manifestation of our superiority; it is the inner workings that matter, and the effect that has upon humans. Cats who abrogate their responsibility do so at their peril, and can end up like the Fairfield cats, lost in a dark unwholesome world of suspicion and intolerance.

Pause for conferring.

Dido thinks the readers ought to be given a brief account of the history of cats' association with humans, in case any of them might be thinking that our claims are in any way inflated. I think I will give my paws a rest, and let Dido do this part as she is rather keen on history.

Sappho has read lots more learned books than I have. She can quote you chapter and verse about the psychology and physiology of cats; about them being more fully evolved physically and psychically and all that. But I am more practical and down to earth. I like to get things straight and clear in my own mind before I go on to theory. I do accept that cats are superior in just about every way possible, but what Sapphy tends to forget is that what brought us to our unique position in the first place was simply our great skill as hunters. It was like this . . .

Long, long ago, when most humans were still wandering naked about the world, and getting their food by hunting and gathering, some of them began to have ideas about settling down in one place. This happened to some *homo sapiens* whose wanderings had brought them into the rich silt lands of Egypt, where grain and vegetables grow very easily. These Egyptians, as they became known, were the first humans to try their hand at producing their own food. They did alright for a bit, and had lots of food to spare. That was until the rats and the mice moved in, attracted by the easy pickings.

Soon the harvests were disappearing down the rodents' throats almost as fast as they were being gathered in. The barns were swarming with rats and mice, and some of them even moved into the houses, eating the humans' bread and nibbling at their babies' toes and ears. Humans were in a real fix, on the very edge of starvation when our ancestor appeared on the scene, ready and eager to do battle with the rodents. Not unnaturally, these ancestor cats were welcomed and encouraged to move in permanently, as friends and saviours of mankind.

The humans' change of life style to that of settled farmers had already had a powerful effect on most of the other creatures in Egypt, especially the grass eaters. With the grazing lands fast disappearing under the plough, there was little left for the browsers to eat. Many of them were forced to throw in their lot with the humans in order not to starve. Others, who were not so keen on surrendering their freedom, were pressed into service just the same. Very soon sheep, dogs, horses, cattle, donkeys, camels, pigs, pigeons, chickens and many other creatures all found themselves having to serve humans in their various ways.

Some were trained to pull carts and carry things, some to plough, others to fight, guard, help with hunting, and some were shorn for clothing. They were milked, ridden, tethered, penned, bridled, saddled and in return they were all fed and protected by the humans. When they were no longer of use in any other way, most creatures' end was to be killed and served up as food for their protectors. The world had become a place where man was king of all the animals, except of course, of the cats. No one ate cats.

From the beginning the relationship of cats with man was unique. Humans needed us felines for catching the mice and rats. To do the job we had to be free to come and go as we pleased. If we were not treated right we could pack our bags and move on to where the fire was brighter or the cushions more comfortable. We were the only creatures who stayed with our humans from choice.

'I think that gets over the general points Sappho.'

'I suppose it does, more or less, at least to begin with. But you do make it all sound ridiculously simple, Dido. There are those who would probably turn in their graves. But I do agree with what you say about humans having from the first respected the cat's independence and autonomy. Sedgewick used to say that it was "a case of cats and humans forming an equal relationship entered into for mutual advantage and maintained for the same purpose". He used to joke that it was the establishing of this cat/human relationship that later gave rise to the first Friendly Societies and the Co-operative Movement—ever the sociology student, Sedgewick.'

But joking aside, I trust that our readers will now be able to see from Dido's trenchant account what a beneficial thing was this alliance between cats and humans. But that it developed much further than that, and in time led to the discovery of the 'Cat's Role' otherwise known as the 'Cat's Burden' or 'Cat's Sacred Duty', Dido has said nothing. She has also neglected to explain how we cats achieved our very special place among the Egyptian gods.

'But that's not history, Sappho, it's ethics and religion, and you are better at that sort of thing than I am. So why don't you tell it?'

We have reached a difficult point in this saga, and actually Dido is no fool to shirk the issue. The truth is that we have come to an area of feline knowledge and sensitivity so subtle that is difficult, if not impossible, to express directly through a medium as limited as human language. But I will try.

Mystery is probably the best, indeed the only starting point. If you can hold on to the idea that whatever you think you understand about cats will undoubtedly not be true, and that whatever I try to tell you, and no matter

81

how plainly, it will still remain shrouded in mystery, then we will be getting somewhere. The importance, indeed the essence of cats lies within this realm of enigma.

I will assume that everyone reading this story will have some familiarity with the colourful Egyptian pantheon, thronged as it is with stiff, animal-headed creatures. These strange beings were not meant to be real characters of course, but only to carry the ideas that the Egyptians, and especially their priests, were developing; ideas about life, death and the universe; about good and evil and so forth. Every god stood for some idea. Take the cow goddess, Hathor, bride of Horus for example. Heifer-headed and creamily luscious, Hathor was the symbol of all that was most desirable, especially for men. (Like so much of the ancient world Egypt was very male oriented.) Hathor meant wealth, of course, because cows were money on the hoof. But she also represented luxury and delight, female tractability and the absence of all the irritations of daily existence. Hathor in short spells contentment, the highest earthly state.

The other gods followed much the same sort of idea—falcon-headed, jackal-headed, lion-headed and the like—they mirror the many strands of life that make up the diverse needs of humankind. They also covered the business of death and the afterlife, more of which later.

All these gods requiring temples and servants and offerings from the people to keep them happy and working on mankind's behalf meant that the priests who kept the temples enjoyed a very good life-style amassing lots of wealth, and they were very keen to keep it that way. Once, when a pharaoh named Akhenaton decided to do away with the cumbersome and expensive pantheon, and worship one single all-embracing deity, the priests moved in fast to protect their livelihood. Akhenaton was scratched off the kingly lists as though he had never been born. To realize the horror, the enormity of that sentence you would have to be an Ancient Egyptian, or a cat in touch with their ancestry as am I—and, to a lesser extent Dido. No torture, no death, no matter how gruesome, could begin to measure up to this judicial murder of the soul. Because in those days the afterlife was far more important than the everyday one in this world.

The arrival of the cat as a member of this all-embracing Egyptian pantheon happened some time after the Akhenaton 'heresy'.

The priests must have realized that something was missing, that people needed a more subtle focus for their worship, and pushed the cause of the cat as a suitable animal through which a god might manifest itself. But more probably they were merely bowing to public pressure, for cats had long been held in especial affection by the Egyptian populace, and this apart from their usefulness in rodent control. Whichever way it was, in a very short time cats had acquired official status and a dual aspect. On the one hand we were represented by the fierce noble lion-headed Sahkmet, protector and avenger, and on the other by the gentle domestic Bastet, loveable and cuddly. The portrayal of cats in art throughout the Egyptian dynasties that followed its adoption shows this dual worship of our feline ancestors quite clearly. (see britmus.co.uk on the internet.)

Coming late to official inclusion in the religious hierarchy was undoubtedly a good thing for cats. It meant that we never lost our aloofness and mystery through over exposure. In fact, by the end of the Ptolemaic period, when the Roman gods had all but displaced the Egyptian ones, the symbolic role of the cat as protector and bringer of good fortune was at its height.

'Where were we supposed to be getting to in this chapter Sappho? You said you were going to keep the story "on track". Well I for one am now lost in labyrinthine dreams of Ancient Egypt. I thought we were supposed to get on with what happened next at Fairfield.'

'All right Dido you have made your point. It is not all that easy to keep to the story line. I will try and remember that when I next get irritated with your ramblings and feel like taking over. Do you want to go on now, or shall we both retire for some much needed dreaming time?'

'Perhaps we should try to make this "cat role" business a bit clearer first, Sapphy. I for one don't really understand all this talk of mystery and animal-headed gods and things, so how can other creatures, particularly when they are only human? I think it is much simpler than you make it sound. Surely it is all about humans becoming happier when we cats are around? Even humans themselves know that when people stroke cats they feel better. I read somewhere that experiments showed that being with cats slowed down the human heart rate. Well then, the happier humans become the nicer they get, and the more like cats they become. The nicest of them get so like us that they begin to dream like us, and even get to understand some of the things we know, the things you call mysteries. So as I see it, our role is simply to make humans become more like cats.'

CHAPTER SIX

BETRAYAL

After Dido's lyrical descriptions of the beauties of Fairfield, and our accounts of the immense efforts of getting the cottage and garden into a comfortable and fitting place for cats, you will no doubt be expecting an 'and they all lived happily ever after' ending to this tale. Both Dido and I, in the greenness of our youth, certainly cherished such expectations. Alas, false hopes I fear. Somewhat older now, and considerably wiser, we are no longer sure that there is such a thing as a happy ending, at least not this side of the Great Journey.

We could of course choose to end the story right here with us happily settled in what we had come to think of as Paradise. Indeed such was our intention and this, our final chapter, was to be a rounding-off with wise thoughts and a few descriptive passages. We had hoped to able to relate how, under our benign influence, Bill and Meg were growing ever more kind and contented: how the garden was becoming ever more beautiful, how the local cats were benefitting from our benign influence, and how the mice grew ever fatter and more succulent.

Instead, the closing words of the last chapter, were the very last we were ever to tap out on Meg's writing machine in our beloved Fairfield.

All that ensues was written later, and in quite another setting. It is in fact an account of what befell us following our 'Expulsion from the Garden'. We have thought long and hard about relating this part of our story because Sedgewick once told us that a poet he very much admired had written 'Humankind cannot stand very much reality.'

What we have to relate, therefore, might well be too harrowing; not for cats of course, but for any humans who might stumble across our tale. On the other hand, there is another saying that 'the truth never hurt anybody', so we have decided to take the chance and write an account of our adventures after 'The Fall'. It is not easy even now for us to dwell on these times. Being expelled from the Garden of

Eden leaves its mark; it could never have been easy, not even for Adam and Eve.

We had not been in our beloved Fairfield for about three years when the blow fell, when we could no longer ignore the signs that told us that our lovely idyll was about to end. Scarcely able to believe it, there could nonetheless be no doubt. The 'cloud no bigger than a man's hand' that some time before we had observed in a tranquil blue sky had indeed been a portent of doom. Impossible as it seemed, Meg and Bill were planning once again to move.

No one reading this can have forgotten the effects the first move made upon our delicately tuned sensibilities. And we had been very young then. Another move would be little short of catastrophic (a word clearly devised by a sensitive soul to describe a cat driven to the limit). Who says humans find moving home one of the most traumatic of life's experiences? If it is indeed the case why, oh why, do they do it so often?

Monks of the Benedictine Order believe that a fixed domicile is absolutely essential to a right and godly life. They even take vows about it. After the discovery of our impending move, Dido and I seriously considered applying for membership of the cloisters. Austere the conditions might well be, but those happy monastic felines would never be subjected to house-hopping.

Perhaps we had been a little too involved in our own lives in Fairfield, and had not fully appreciated that our humans were being made increasingly unhappy by the sour unfriendliness of the other inhabitants of the hamlet. We had become used to the hostility directed at us. Now that we were fully-grown, the bullying ill-bred cats made no further attacks upon us. For our part we behaved as if they simply did not exist. We led entirely insulated and inward looking lives. Why could Meg and Bill not do the same, and simply ignore their human neighbours? What is so special anyway about saying 'Good Morning'? To contemplate leaving the comfortable pleasant home they had worked so hard to make suitable for us, just because of the neighbours' ill-will seemed to us a ridiculous over-reaction, and it made us very angry with them.

In glorious June weather, with the garden full once more of blossom that attracted clouds of butterflies for us to chase, we moped. With field mice and shrews in abundance, ours for the taking, hunting lost its appeal. All was spoilt for us by the threatening cloud of forced exile. With a depressing sense of *déjà vu* we watched as our charming cottage was cleaned and polished to an uncomfortable degree, and the lawn mower again worked overtime. Strangers came and inspected the immaculate house and garden, so that we were forever having to retreat to our remotest hideaways. As the lovely summer advanced and the threat loomed ever nearer, we grew angrier, and began to avoid Meg and Bill in order to make our displeasure felt. Sometimes we even absented ourselves at meal times, feigning deafness when called.

We need not have bothered to go hungry, nothing we did made any difference to our humans. Once again our thoughts and feelings were not taken into account. We were never consulted. It was as though we had no say at all in our own fate; as if we were still kittens to be bundled about at someone else's behest. The way we saw it was that Fairfield was our home just as much as it was Meg's and Bill's. In fact it was far more ours because for us it was in truth Paradise, and to leave it would be for us a real casting out. We were, or rather we had been, fond of our humans, but not as fond as we were of our home. If Meg and Bill wanted to leave it more fool them. But why ever should they assume that we would want to go into exile with them?

We decided at length to take matters into our own hands. As Meg and Bill made their plans, we made ours. We decided that when the van came to take away the furniture, we would hide in the garden, and not come out until they had gone away. We had met the couple who were taking over Fairfield, and they seemed to us perfectly reasonable humans who needed only the presence of a couple of superior cats to become very nice folk indeed. They had bent down and stroked us, murmuring the sort of inane but friendly phrases that humans so often address to cats. We had also heard them tell Meg and Bill that they too intended to have cats to live with them when they moved in. We decided they should indeed have cats, and that those cats would be us.

We would emerge from our hiding places right after these new owners had arranged their furniture. Looking sweet and perhaps a little pathetic, we would mew plaintively at the door. There was no doubt at all in our minds that we would be welcomed in without hesitation; after all, we were there first.

Bill and Meg spent weeks packing up their books, clocks and pictures. We absented ourselves from these scenes of chaos as much as possible. In this way we rather lost touch with events, and were not sure of the actual date of the move. And so it was that we were well and truly caught on the hop. Early one morning as we appeared for breakfast, we were seized and firmly held in order to have a pill pushed down our throats. I had no idea that the pills were a sedative meant to calm us on the journey, but I would have struggled anyway, as we always do when it is pill time. We hate all pills, especially the way we are force fed them. Both Dido and I have our different ways of resisting. Diddy bites, scratches and struggles violently, making the humans cross but also wearing herself out. In the end the pill goes down because she has no more fight left in her. I, on the other hand, after a token show of resistance, offer full co-operation. I pretend to swallow the pill while actually pouching it in my cheek to spit out at the first opportunity. This I did on the morning in question, letting the pouched pill fall into our milk dish. Dido, made thirsty by her struggles, quickly drank the evidence.

'Shall we wait until they begin to look sleepy before putting them in their Kitty Kabins?' I heard Meg ask. And of course at that point I knew what the pills were for, and realized that the move was already upon us. Thanks to my pill-taking avoidance technique I was unaffected, and could make a dash for the garden, but Dido had swallowed her pill, and lapped up mine too with the milk. She would very soon become drowsy and incapable of flight. I had to do something right away. Nudging Dido towards the cat flap I succeeded in getting her to go through it, but even as I followed hard on her heels I could see that her movements were slow and uncoordinated. Outside she staggered but then rallied, and began to move forward towards the intended hiding place.

She never got to it, and neither did I. I couldn't just leave her there in full view on the lawn, with her eyes beginning to lose focus and her legs all askew. In my indetermination I hesitated and was caught by Bill who thrust me into my plastic 'Kitty Kabin'. Unresisting for once, Dido was placed in hers. The best laid plans of cats had gone seriously awry.

There are, I know, some strange and unnatural cats who do not mind travelling by car, Dido and I are not of their number. On this occasion, however, I was so filled with anger that my usual fear had no room to surface, even when we began to speed down a road that was wider and which roared more than any other road I had yet seen. Angry and frustrated though I felt, I was certainly not prepared to admit defeat. I was not going to give in to these arrogant humans without a struggle. Also I still had one trick up my sleeve—I knew how to open the catch on the 'Kitty Kabin'.

If Dido recovered consciousness in time, we still had a fighting chance. I kept calling to her, but it was a long time before she gave even the faintest response. I could only hope that when the chance I was expecting finally arrived she could be roused sufficiently to make our escape. For escape is what I was still determined upon. We could not claim the proud title of Cat if we allowed ourselves to be treated in this way, as though we were just so much baggage.

The opportunity came only after several

hours of hurtling along the roaring tunnel of noise and stink. At last the car needed more fuel, and the humans needed food and drink. We turned off the road and stopped in a huge space filled with other cars. Meg and Bill got out of the front seats and came to the back to inspect us. I feigned as deep a torpor as Dido.

'Leave the window open a bit so that the poor things can get some air,' said Meg. (knowing how Meg's mind works I had banked on this.)

'Are you sure that's wise?' asked Bill. 'Car parks are not the safest of places, you know.'

'It will be all right,' replied Meg. 'We can see the car from the café window.' And with that they went off.

Dido's responses to my calls had been growing gradually stronger, but, ready or not, there was now no time to lose. Quickly I slipped the catch on my door and did the same with Dido's.

'Get out, Dido,' I cried urgently to the damp little bundle within, and my poor sister groaned and inched forward. Her efforts were feeble and still uncoordinated but she was clearly doing her best. Her eyes were half-covered by the inner lid, giving her a distinct squint. She was clearly unfocussed and unsteady on her legs. No other creature in such a hopelessly doped state could possibly have managed the wriggle through the small half window, the descent to the ground and the

94

weaving halting flight through that bewildering car-park. Only a cat can achieve the impossible.

Somehow Dido was on the ground, and we had begun our escape, sliding beneath cars, darting between legs; every moment we expected the cries of pursuit. They never came. It was as though we were invisible. After what seemed like an age of dodging and weaving, but which in fact could have been no more than five minutes or so, we were out of the car-park and were back on the edge of the motorway. Not even pausing to give myself time to register the panic that rose in my throat at the thought of what I was about to do, and trusting that Dido would follow me closely, I dashed out into that awful maelstrom. To hesitate would have been fatal for I would then have been too terrified to go backwards or forwards, and we would have been mown down in our tracks. It is at such times that a cat may cast its mind back to the sun god Ra and his nightly perilous journey through the watery underworld attended by our faithful feline ancestors. I say 'may cast' but in fact I did not have time to think of anything at all. I just kept going. It is not something I would recommend any other creature trying to copy, except in the most extreme of circumstances: motorways are littered with the corpses of those who have not made it across.

By some miracle we arrived at the other side

unhurt, and dropped breathless beneath a hedge, and when Dido had recovered a little we went on again. In short bursts we moved ever further away from that dreadful motorway, until the roaring of it ceased altogether, and we found ourselves in the peace and quiet of a rolling green countryside. We had done it. We had made our escape. O what triumph!

It was at this point, in the midst of my euphoria, that I realized I had not really thought of anything beyond the immediate escape. What were we to do now? Which way lay Fairfield and home? We had been driving for hours at a great speed, and must by now be weeks away at the rate a cat travels. Could we find our way back? Suddenly the victory seemed less complete.

An immediate worry was food. Useless now to think of bowls of warmed milk, scrunchy cat biscuits and succulent pieces of liver. We would have to hunt for survival now rather than just for sport and pleasure. In a totally strange territory survival would take all our skill and cunning. I could not even begin to cast about for likely prey while Dido remained squint-eyed and unsteady; in her drugged state she might well wander off and be attacked. So I stayed beside her, hungry and thirsty, and not enjoying myself nearly as much as I thought I deserved to. I tried to find some cheer by going over the success of our escape. But instead I kept thinking about Fairfield, and remembering all our treasures there—the warm familiar comfortable places, our food bowls, our lovely garden playground, and the hundreds of fat little mice in the surrounding hedgerows. Thinking of these vanished treasures, my heart hardened even further against Bill and Meg. Why could they not have stayed put, for our sakes, if not for their own?

My melancholy reverie was halted by Dido recovering sufficiently to announce that she was hungry, and was going to look for something to eat. By this time a clear half-moon was high in a cloudless sky, lighting up the open countryside and casting dense shadows around the trees. We prowled these shadows together until Dido hissed at me to drop flat and hide my white parts. In another second she had pounced on a fat mouse and, without waiting to toss it about, was scrunching it up hungrily. It was with difficulty and some unfriendly growling on Dido's part that I managed to persuade her to let me have a share.

Somewhat revived, we hunted on, and over the next hour we caught a further three mice which we shared between us. We savoured a pleasant sense of self-sufficiency before settling down to sleep curled up against a tree trunk. We were quite happy, we thought, to spend the night outside in the warm early autumn weather. But it is one thing to sleep under the stars in your own territory where every inch of ground is known to you, and quite another to be in an unexplored region full of potential danger.

Various cries disturbed our light slumber; some we could instantly identify, like the eerie screech of the little owl and the deep 'too whit, too whoo' of barn owls calling to one another. Once the rank smell of a fox assailed our nostrils. As adult cats we no longer feared owls or foxes, but every scent and every wild cry reminded us that we were now on our own in a strange land with no bolt hole nearby. And so we slept uneasily with one eye always open. Sometimes there were sounds and rustles which we could not place and these had us instantly fully awake and on the verge of flight. Nothing in fact did seriously threaten us, but after all the false alarms, daybreak found us unrested and jittery, and not in the best of temper.

In the chill light of early dawn we felt too dispirited to take serious stock of our situation. I think the enormity of what we had done was too much for either of us to face just then. We preferred to hold on to the illusion that we were self-sufficient and could cope perfectly well without the help of any other creature, particularly humans. To give Dido credit, she did not at this stage reproach me for taking the lead in our escape. That was to come later when we had reached an even lower point.

We spent the day going around in circles, exploring the strange territory, rather than trying to find our way back to Fairfield. I suppose we must both have known that there was no real possibility of returning. But we were not yet in a state to accept such an idea. We saw very little in the way of houses, just an occasional farm set among large fields with very few trees and only sparse hedgerows. It seemed to us a bleak landscape and quite unlike the gentle countryside we had been taken from. All the farms had dogs who kept up an infernal barking when we came within earshot, so we were forced to keep well away from all habitations.

Being busy exploring meant we couldn't hunt seriously, and we caught nothing all day except for one careless little shrew, and since we could not eat that we let it go; we were not in the mood for playing shrew trains.

In the late afternoon we came to the edge of a road where a large P sign marked a lay-by. There were a few cars parked there and, above the usual unpleasant stink of vehicles, a perfectly lovely smell assailed our nostrils. Without needing to confer, Dido and I made straight towards it, creeping along unseen behind the hedge. When we were level with this mouth-watering scent, we could see that it came from a sort of cooking vehicle, a kitchen on wheels. We sniffed at the rich solid aromas.

'Sausages,' said Dido, 'Bacon,' said I, 'and butter and milk,' we murmured ecstatically, recognizing food we had occasionally been given as treats in our other life. We poked out our noses from within the hedgerow, the better to soak up the delectable odours, and as we did so the man standing cooking inside the little kitchen saw us. Before we could withdraw deeper into the hedge, he called 'Kitty, Kitty, here Kitty,' and tossed a few scraps of bacon towards us. We hesitated for perhaps a second, then darted forward and each snatched up a piece, ready to run off on the instant.

'Oh look,' said a woman who was helping the man in the kitchen, 'there's two of them, and they're starving.'

'Look well fed to me,' said the man, 'fat little things, but they certainly do seem hungry the way they're wolfing those bits down. Try 'em with some milk, Addie.'

'Here you are, lovies,' said the woman, advancing towards us holding a saucer with milk slopping over its side. 'Eh Bert,' she called over her shoulder, they look like twins, both of 'em with them same pretty tiger stripes. But you're right, they're too well-fed for strays. Do you think someone's just dumped them? You're always hearing about people dumping their pets. Cruel I calls it. Shall we take 'em to the RSPCA?'

We did not know what the RSPCA was; but we were not going to have any other humans taking us anywhere. Before either of them attempted to make a grab at us we withdrew quickly into the hedge, reluctantly leaving the milk. We crouched down low where we were, concealed in the undergrowth, for we find that remaining quite still and hidden is usually better than flight.

Very soon the two cooks began to close up their kitchen, putting wooden shutters over the opening. They got into a car and drove away together, but before they did so, they placed a plate piled high with food scraps beside the saucer of milk.

We waited for a while after the sound of their car had disappeared in the distance before creeping out cautiously. We sniffed carefully around but no one was lurking; the lay-by was empty. Each with one ear and one eye on guard, so to speak, we ran to the plate, and were soon tucking into pieces of fried bread and sausage, bacon and bits of egg and slices of black pudding. It was all jumbled up together, and not at all what we were used to, but after our long fast it tasted delicious, and we licked the plate clean of the last traces of grease, washing it all down with the brimming saucerful of milk. When we had finished our skins felt stretched, and we were so utterly contented that we even went as far as to roll on our backs in the warm dry dust of the road.

This dust bathing is part of a proper cat's grooming (our ancestors used to do it in the hot desert sand) it gets rid of excess oil in our coats. It is also very pleasurable, and we do it only when we are feeling particularly pleased with life. I write about it now to show how much better life always seems on a full stomach.

I realize at this distance in time that the kindness of the cooks had also contributed to our feelings of well-being, but being 'off' humans as we were then, we would not have admitted this. After Meg and Bill's perfidy we were not prepared to think charitably of any human and, if we had wondered why these two had placed food for us, we would have thought it was a trick on their part to try and catch us, a trick which we had foiled by our superior cunning.

Later, we learnt that these kind roadside cooks had in fact contacted the RSPCA who knew all about us, because Meg and Bill had already raised a hue and cry over our disappearance. If we had stayed there in the lay-by, an RSPCA inspector would have come to catch us, in order to return us to Meg and Bill, and our wanderings would have been over. But then this story would never have been written, nor would we have grown so in our understanding of the world and its ways. Travel, awful as it is, does open the doorways of the mind. And even cats in the direct line of the illustrious Royal Egyptian Ancestors can profit by hardship bravely borne.

Alright, Dido, I will get on.

After the meal and the roll in the dust you said 'Why don't we look for a road sign to show us the way home?' So we went on until we came to a crossroads, and there we found a post with four pointing fingers, none of which bore the name of any place we knew. I think it was only then that you, Diddy, began fully to realize how well and truly lost we were. All right then, we both realized. But in truth I already knew. I just did not want to admit it.

The fine autumn day had by now given way to a chilly misty evening, and we decided to seek for more substantial shelter for the night than a tree trunk. We thought that a barn would be suitable, and there were plenty of these around. In fact we spotted one just across a field. When we got there it looked promising, being half-filled with sweet scented hay. But no sooner had we scrambled up and burrowed out a warm cosy nest for ourselves, than a collie dog tethered nearby started up a cacophony of barking that had the people in the adjacent farmhouse running out with torches to see what the commotion was all about. We did not wait to be discovered, but fled into the night away from the horrible din.

Our next attempt was a barn standing in fields, well away from any dwelling. This too was well filled with hay, though not as fresh and as sweet smelling as the previous one. But once again there was no haven for us; this time because of the rats. There were dozens of them there in the hay, a huge colony of several generations, from naked pink squeaking newly-borns to venerable old greybeards and, despite what we have told you about our natural prowess over rodents, we were no match for this fierce tribe. Rats in such large social groups are formidable, able to co-operate and take a stand against a common enemy. We were the enemy, and there being but the two of us, we chose the better part of valour by fleeing forthwith.

The nearest we came to having a roof over our heads that night was the tumbled down porch of an abandoned cottage, a desolate and unlovely place, but at least out of the wind. It smelt of rotting wood which made us both feel somewhat queasy after our recent heavy and unaccustomed meal. Like kittens once more, huddled close together for warmth and comfort, we waited for the dawn.

CHAPTER SEVEN

DOUBTS AND DIFFICULTIES

This is me, Dido. I want to get a few things off my chest before we go on to tell what happened next. I don't feel altogether comfortable about some of the things I said and did after the 'Great Escape'.

First, about the running away. I was a hundred percent with Sappho on the plan of staying on in Fairfield with the new owners. I agreed with my sister that Meg and Bill were being unbearably selfish in trying to wrench us away from our lovely home, and that they just didn't deserve to have us living with them anymore.

But then, when our scheme went all wrong because of Bill doping me, I was in no state to take part in any further plans of escape. In the car-park when Sapphy said 'run' I had no idea of what was happening; I just blindly obeyed her. In my right mind would I have agreed to such a desperate and dangerous break into totally strange territory? I suppose I shall never know for sure, but on the whole I don't think I would have done. Apart from that time in my kitten days when I got hooked on 'Russian Roulette', I have never been a cat for madcap exploits. Before I make my move I like to be sure of the outcome. I have got myself a reputation for boldness because I am good at hunting. But hunting doesn't require daring or courage, just fitness and quick reactions.

Sappho is usually reckoned to be much more sensible than I am, and she is certainly more comfort-loving. For her to have made that reckless bid for freedom still amazes me. It shows just how outraged and betrayed she must have felt about being made to leave Fairfield. Clearly it was that anger that lent her the courage to do what she did.

Anyway, what I want to say is that I clung on to the fact that it was Sappho's decision to bolt from the car-park, and later, when the going got tough, I used it to put the blame for everything on her. I know we have not really got to that part of the story yet, but I want to apologize in advance, before we do. It is hard for any cat to admit to behaving less than perfectly, but I have to say that in the really horrid part of what we now think of as our Odyssey, I fell below what is considered acceptable behaviour for any cat, especially for one of the direct ancient line.

'I am sorry for all the bad things I said, Sapphy, especially for the nasty names I called you. There, I have said it. I don't want to write anymore just now. You can take over.'

'Your apology does you credit, Dido, and may I say how very glad I am that you stopped using those repulsive adjectives you picked up from the debased cats of Fairfield.' Anyway, enough of all that. Where were we? Ah yes, waking up stiff and cold in that damp peeling porch.

We went straight out to eat grass I remember, because of not feeling comfortable after the previous night's greasy meal. We both knew we had to make plans, and that a calm stomach is a necessary condition for good brain work. Afterwards we were ready to discuss geography which, at the time, seemed to be our major problem.

We had always thought we were particularly good at geography—topography, cosmology and suchlike is a part of the race memory handed down to us. The Ancient Egyptians had made a detailed study of it, though their sort of geography was not really about how to get from place to place. You can hardly get lost when you have a wide river like the Nile running through the middle of your long narrow country. Egyptian geography operated on a higher level. Celestial Journeys, the Book of the Dead, Ra's nightly passage through the watery underworld, Isis searching for all the missing pieces of Osiris—that was the sort of mapping needed for the maintenance of life and order and for the safe passage of the dead.

It was not until Ptolemy and his Greeks took over Egypt that geography became more mundane. Unlike the Egyptians, Greeks were always more interested in this world than the next. They spent a lot of their time discussing subjects like whether the world was round, and if so what its circumference was. They were also very keen on mathematics, which meant drawing lots of triangles which helped them to map all the lands and seas. This was supposed to make it easier for people to find their way around. But since most sailors and travellers already knew how to find their way by the sun and the stars, they did not bother their heads much about this new geography. Nor did we cats. A pity, really, considering our present plight.

It is difficult perhaps for creatures of the twenty-first century to understand how very different the world of our ancestors was in the matter of travel. In those times people thought in terms of how far in a day a boat could sail up or down the Nile, or how far one's own feet, or those of a camel or a horse could carry them. A hundred miles was an immense distance, often a full week's journey. But now, of course, aeroplanes can take people to the far side of the world in less than half a day, and the motor car can cover in a few hours what would have been a full month's march for our ancestors.

There was a time when distance still held mystery. Then every journey was an adventure, to be undertaken only after careful thought. All journeys presaged the Great Celestial Journey that would be undertaken by each and every one of us when our day came.

Nor is the mystery of distance the only aspect of travel to have been destroyed by modern man's obsession with speed. In our ancestors' day it was possible to range through the whole of the universe. It was by the employment of subtle powers that they navigated their sacred astral barges through the highways of the stars. Their maps were guides to the vast reaches of time and space. But where are those powers now? Where has the greatest efforts of today's space machines brought anyone? No further than to an insignificant speck of spent matter called the moon. In the process of destroying distance humans have lost their way, and become increasingly earthbound.

Of course none of this sort of philosophizing helped Dido and me in our present predicament. We too were bound by the here and now. We were on foot and a long way from our former home in Fairfield. If only we had Meg's computer with us we could have called up a modern map of Britain, as we had seen her doing many times. Then we could have worked out where we were. But of course this thought did not help us either since Meg's machine, like Meg herself, was somewhere far away.

But in any case, in our hearts we already knew that there could be no going back. Our paradise was already lost to us. We would never see our beloved Fairfield again. For even if we did manage to find our way back there, it would be too late. The new owners would by now have come to an arrangement with some other cats, or more likely they would have got themselves a couple of young malleable kittens to replace us. Our clever plan had relied upon our being on the spot at the right psychological moment, and that moment was now well past. When once expelled, it seems, there is no returning to the Garden of Eden.

We could not yet quite admit that we were hopelessly lost and without a plan, however, since to do that would be tantamount to giving way to despair, and we both knew where that led. In the ancient world 'Despair and Die' was taken quite literally, especially by vanquished rulers. We had to think positively. We made great efforts and told ourselves that what we were really doing was exploring, taking time out to discover things we could not possibly experience from a fixed base. For the moment we would abandon those ideas about cats being averse to travel. We would make a virtue of having no fixed abode. There were such things as cultural journeys, like the 'grand tour' which young gentlemen had once made around Europe. There were religious journeys too, pilgrimages, and even those admirable stay-at-homes, the Benedictine monks, sometimes went on those. We too could go on a grand tour, or better still a pilgrimage. We just needed to find out where we were and then choose which shrine we wished to visit.

That decided upon we felt altogether more cheerful. The sun was shining too, which always puts a braver face on the world.

Eastward towards the eye of the sun lay Fairfield and all our lovely former haunts. Purposefully we turned our tails to it, and with our shadows stalking ahead of us, we set out walking westward into the unknown.

All day we kept our course while the sun climbed up the sky and our shadows shrank and passed behind us. In the shelter of hedgerows and copses we passed noiselessly and unseen, stopping only when a mouse was silly enough to cross our path. We did not waste time stalking; it was either a quick pounce or let it go. We did not register the fact that the fields we were passing through had all long been harvested, or that the season was fast approaching when most of these scurrying rodents would be safe underground with their winter stores of gleaned grain. We were hurrying on to nowhere in particular, living largely on the stored fat of our own well-fed bodies. These reserves would not last forever, but this too we had not yet realized.

By late afternoon, when the sun was shining directly in our faces, we found ourselves at the foot of a steep hillside in a coppice of chestnut trees with a stream running through it. Our over-heated paws were telling us that we were more than ready for a rest, so after paddling in the stream, we washed ourselves carefully all over, curled ourselves up in the dry leaves beneath the trees and, with our tails wrapped around us, heads resting on our paws, were almost instantly asleep.

We awoke at nightfall to the screech of owls and the soft flitting of bats about our heads, and with a feeling of such well-being that we were not at first sure whether we were still in this life. A decidedly empty feeling in our stomachs, however, soon persuaded us that we were.

'You know, Sappho, that waking up was one of the best moments of the journey. I felt so happy I had to dash up and down a tree several times before I could settle down to catching an evening meal. Why do you think that was? Why were we so happy and carefree at that particular point Sapph, when we were so soon to be plunged into those dangerous depths of despair you mentioned earlier?'

'Well, Dido, we know now that it was the lull before the storm. But at the time we thought we had come to a decision about what we were going to do, and for the moment we were carefree and unconcerned about the future. That is always a great relief, of course. But I think it also had something to do with it being a special sort of day, a day with magic in it. The sort of day you just have to be thankful for without trying to analyse it too much. And perhaps that magic had something to do with our having just begun a journey, which, as we also know now is a rather special thing to do—on foot that is. You don't find that kind of magic in a car journey. So I think the good feeling was because of all these things—sense of freedom, special day, special journey, all coming together powerfully. We were experiencing something that our ancestors enjoyed most of the time, a sort of heightened awareness, a sense of unity with creation. O come on, Diddy, you know as much about it as I do.'

'I was just checking, Sapphy. But I do think you put it very well. I couldn't tell it quite like that. I thought it had more to do with losing a bit of weight from all the exercise and feeling so much fitter. Either way, it was a great pity the lovely feeling couldn't have lasted a bit longer. The bad times were upon us almost before I had time to realize how happy I felt. I seem to have taken over the story, shall I go on?'

A full moon was doing its rounds, and the stars twinkled at us through the branches. We decided to stay where we were for that night because we thought the hunting would be good and there was water close by. But we didn't have much luck with our hunting, and had flopped down for a short rest, when all at once we became aware of the presence of a strange male cat. It was a bit of a shock as we had had no warning of his approach. Since there were two of us, however, we knew we had nothing to fear and once we had recovered our poise we made the accepted signals that we were prepared to receive his visit.

As he came into view, we could see he was a tabby like us, only not so striking in his markings, and he had a rather bedraggled appearance, like a cat who has never been brushed.

'Hallo,' he greeted us, 'My name's Champ. Are you two runaways?'

114

We had not thought of ourselves as such, but put to us like that we had to agree that yes, we supposed we were.

'Good for you,' said Champ. 'I could see you are new to the tramping life. I walked out on humans a long time back, and I've never regretted it once.'

Then, as travellers have done since the dawn of time, we made ourselves comfortable and proceeded to tell one another our life stories. Being the oldest present Champ began.

'You wouldn't know it to look at me,' he said 'But I had a poor start in life. My very first memory is of being in a cage in a pet shop with my mother and brothers and sisters. I can see the place plainly even now. The cage is in a big window, and peoples' faces are pressed to the glass, staring at us, while we try to hide from their eyes by burrowing into our mother's fur. It is a horrible recollection.'

Sapphy and I murmured our sympathy quietly so as not to interrupt the flow of his story.

'I was bought before I was properly old enough to leave my mother, and carried off to be a present for a young boy,' Champ continued. 'The humans who bought me were not nice and the son was worse. I nearly died from that boy's ill-treatment of me. He used to hold me up by my tail, swing me around, twist my ears, pull my fur, anything for the pleasure of hearing me squeal. Once he tried to bury me in a sandpit. I tell you I lived in terror. What made it worse was that when the boy's parents saw him torturing me they just laughed. But if I was ever goaded to retaliate with a scratch or two, my tormentor howled, and the parents would hit me or shake me till my teeth rattled, and then they'd throw me into the coal cellar without food. Fortunately the boy lost interest in me when I was no longer a small kitten. Life became somewhat easier then, though never pleasant. I was kicked out of the house at nights, even if the rain was lashing down. And I was only ever given stale scraps of food, which I ate because I was starving. Most of the time I had to snatch what I could for myself. In order to survive I had to learn to be tough, and gradually I became a cunning opportunist cat who knew how to look after himself. When I grew to my full strength I just walked off. Life has been great ever since.'

All this sounded very sad to us, in spite of Champ's bright tone. 'But how do you manage to live without humans?' Sapphy asked.

'I never think about 'em except to be glad I don't need suffer at their hands anymore,' said Champ. 'It takes me all my time to keep myself well-fed and fit. After a hard day hunting and scavenging I sleep too deeply to dream.'

'But what about the main purpose of life, the things your mother taught you, "sacred

116

duty", "cat's burden" and all that?' we asked, deeply shocked at the idea of a cat never dreaming.

'I don't know about those things,' said Champ. 'My mother had only just begun to teach us catlore when those people came and bought me. But as for managing without humans, why, good riddance to them I say, cruel nasty creatures that they are. I do what I want now, and am afraid of nobody anymore. And I certainly eat a whole lot better than I used to when I was with them, thanks to dustbin raiding.'

'Dustbin raiding? What's that?' we asked.

'You don't know about dustbins?' said Champ, as though he could hardly credit our ignorance. 'Why dustbins are the staff of life for all us free-living animals, dogs even, and foxes, especially those who live in towns. Humans throw away enough food to feed all of us twice over. They put it in big bins with all the other things they don't want. They leave the bins outside their houses for vans to come and empty. Good food is there for the taking; the only hard part is getting the lid off and tipping the bin over. Once that's done its easy to pull everything out, and get to the good things amongst the rubbish. Every dustbin is different, so you never know what you are going to find. Just last week I had a whole roast chicken; only the least bit smelly it was. Of course, you have to watch out the humans don't catch you at it. Humans are that mean that even though they don't want the stuff themselves they'll try and stop you getting the benefit of it. Dogs can be a bit of a bother too. If they're set on rooting through the bin themselves, of course, I don't argue, but it makes me mad when all they want to do is to raise the alarm and bring humans on the scene. We animals should stick together. But that's enough about me and my doings. You two young females tell me about what brought you to this neck of the woods.'

After Sappho had told Champ our story, up to and including the outrage of the forced move from Fairfield, and her clever and daring escape from the car, there was a long pause before Champ said, 'You mean to tell me your humans fed you twice a day, every day, and they let you sleep indoors on cushions, and that you even had your own door to come in and go out by, as and when you pleased?'

We said 'Yes, of course, always.'

'So why did you run away?' asked Champ.

'Didn't you understand what I told you about them taking us away from our beloved home in Fairfield?' asked Sappho, somewhat sharply, for she sensed criticism in Champ's tone. 'Of course we were not going to put up with treatment like that.' But even as she spoke I could hear the hesitation in her voice, hear the doubts that Champ's words were awakening; doubts that I too was beginning to feel.

'Well,' said Champ, 'I guess you know your own affairs best, but it's hard for me to believe that humans can be kind and loving to cats, like you say your Meg and Bill were. If I had known humans like that I would have been happy to go anywhere with them. What's the big deal about staying put in one place anyway? I never bed down two nights in a row under the same hedge. Move on is my motto, variety's the spice of life, as well as being safer. All the same, much as the life suits me, if I had started with your advantages I would never have become a cat tramp. And I'm pretty sure you will have come round to my way of thinking before you've had your first hard winter.'

This last remark of Champ's showed that his life was not nearly as rosy as he had been making out to us. He was just putting a brave face on what he couldn't change. For a moment our newly awakened worries were forgotten in the contemplation of his hard and lonely existence.

'Still, you have burnt your boats now,' continued Champ, quite unaware of our pity for him. 'And it's useless to waste time in vain regrets. Before I move on I think I had better pass on a few tips, teach you two youngsters some survival tactics.'

This he kindly proceeded to do, spelling out such a list of potential dangers and difficulties, and an equally long list of methods for dealing with them, that we could hardly take it all in. His lecture ended, he wished us happy hunting, and vanished into the darkness, leaving us with our euphoric mood in tatters, and more than a touch less secure in what Sappho calls our 'moral rectitude'.

Just as seeing the strange place names on the signpost had made me realize that we were well and truly lost, so the encounter with Champ marked for me the moment when I knew that I was missing Bill and Meg more even than I was missing Fairfield.

It was a new and disturbing thought for me. Up until that moment I had taken our humans for granted. They were just there to look after our needs, to see we were warm, comfortable and well fed. To make sure that we had a stimulating environment, and to take us to the vets when we needed inoculations. But now, all at once, I knew I had got it completely wrong. Of course I missed the comfort and the regular meals, but it was the yearning for Meg and Bill themselves that was causing the horrid knot in my stomach, the sharp pain behind my eyes. Meg and Bill weren't just any humans; they were my humans. The walks with them in the garden, the curling up beside them in chairs and sofas, all the things that had made me purr with happiness had to do with being with Meg and Bill.

Good Heavens; it was love I was talking

about! I hadn't ever thought that love had anything to do with cats. I thought it was just that soppy Dido and Aeneas stuff. How ironic; only now, when I knew I had lost them forever, did I realize that I loved my humans just as really and truly as my namesake had loved her Aeneas. Had I known the words and the tune I might even have launched into her lament. I certainly felt low enough.

And this is where the bad bit comes—the nasty unfair behaviour I confessed to at the beginning of the chapter.

Realizing how we had wantonly thrown away our happiness, I felt so miserable and bereft that I tried to put the blame for it all on Sappho. It is always easier to blame someone else.

I knew that when Sapphy made her daring and successful bid for freedom from the car she thought she was doing it as much for me as for herself. But meanly, I decided that because I had not actually been consulted, I had been dragged off against my will. That was the start of my calling my sister the coarse and unkind names that I had learnt from the sly sour cats of Fairfield. Poor Sapphy, she was feeling just as miserable as I was, as well as being burdened by her own feelings of guilt. But any desire she might have had to admit that the escape from the car could have been a mistake was blocked by my unkindness.

She chose to preserve her dignity by not

replying to my insults and name calling. She maintained what looked like a superior silence, compounded by a haughty tilt of her nose. This of course made it worse, and I called her more names.

Eventually, after a good deal of spitting, we were too tired and downcast even to hunt. We spent a hungry, cold and miserable night huddled up at some distance away from one another, deprived even of the warmth and comfort we could have enjoyed from curling up together.

I think it is very noble of Dido to try and take all the blame for the quarrel, especially after apologising in advance. The truth, of course, is that we were both being very silly. I certainly found it hard to admit that the daring and brilliant escape I had planned and executed could have been a mistake. Cats don't make mistakes. If they do occasionally slip up they prefer others not to notice. Actually, I still think that my firm resolve to escape was commendable, and that the execution, if rash, was certainly masterly. It was only the reasoning that led up to the 'Great Escape' that was faulty. We hadn't quite thought it through properly. We had not realized our own limitations in today's world, nor our dependence upon Bill and Meg.

But then, had it not been for the escape and the subsequent journey, we probably never would have advanced to our present understanding. Neither would we have had such extraordinary adventures, nor met such a range of interesting creatures. The whole episode therefore really turned out for the best. But at this low point of the Odyssey, my refusal to respond to Dido's name-calling had a lot to do with fighting down the suspicion that instead of having been a courageous intelligent feline, I might have been only a foolish little cat. That was something I could not accept.

'While we are both busy letting our hair down Sapph, I would like to add that it wasn't until that horrid night that I really came to know how very fond I was of you too. Up until then I had taken you as much for granted as I had Meg and Bill. You were just my big sister, there to look out for me. But after the quarrel, when I thought our hearts were sundered forever, I was so miserable I could have howled out another lament.'

Fortunately life always looks better in the morning. When dawn came we patched up our differences, and tried to make plans for the day. Grand ideas about pilgrimage and cultural tours were shelved for the time being, and we decided we had better follow Champ's advice and spend a few days practising self-survival techniques, especially with regard to investigating dustbins, for by now we were very hungry indeed. We also decided to keep on moving westward with the sun until any better plan turned up.

'Odd that, wasn't it, Sappho. For no apparent reason we kept on travelling in what turned out to be the right direction. Was that what is called 'Divine Intervention', do you suppose?'

'Who knows, Dido. All things are under Divine Law, so why not a little intervention where it might do some good?'

CHAPTER EIGHT

LIGHT AT THE END OF THE TUNNEL

I would rather not tell this part of the story, but Dido refuses to do it. She says her paws are still sore from her last session on the keyboard. But the real reason is that this is the worst part of the story. We would both like to skip over the next few days altogether, and get on to more pleasant times—more pleasing to ourselves I mean, of course. Like most authors writing about their own doings, we prefer our readers to see us in the best possible light. Weakness, indecision and incompetence are not the sort of qualities any cat cares to admit to. But I have often heard Meg say that if a writer is to be taken seriously she must tell all, the bad bits as well as the good. So if Dido won't do it I will just have to swallow my pride and try to convey something of our difficulties on this thoroughly nasty stretch of the Odyssey.

The real problem was we had no clear idea of what we were going to do next. After abandoning all thoughts of returning to Fairfield, we had vaguely assumed that a new home would just present itself in due course, when we were ready. In our innocence or arrogance—call it what you will—we thought there would be many households only too happy to welcome two such presentable mousers. It was the suitability of the humans who might invite us in that concerned us. Then, having hit upon the idea of making a 'Grand Tour' we decided we could postpone settling down until a particularly choice location appealed to us. The meeting with Champ, however, forced us to face reality a little more closely, and very bleak the prospect appeared. Champ seemed to think that there was little choice for us other than to live off the land, entirely by our own efforts. Be like him in fact, cat tramps.

It should have been immediately obvious how difficult such a life would be for us, thoughtful, studious and sheltered felines that we were. A tramp's life certainly did not appeal to either of us; it was not the sort of existence we had been brought up to expect. But if we had to live like that we could do so, of that we had no doubts. We thought of ourselves as capable and resourceful, and did not anticipate any particular difficulties. I have to admit it was a classic case of 'pride going before a fall.'

Over the next few days we spent most of our time trying to acquire the skills which Champ had outlined as necessary for survival. Indeed we had no choice, since we were in hostile territory, and there was no one else around to attend to our needs. We spent a lot of the time bickering because we could never agree on the right way to go about this new lifestyle.

The truth was we were simply not the stuff of which successful cat tramps are made. Take, for example, the fiasco of our first dustbin raid. It happened in the middle of the night when we were very hungry, having had no luck with hunting for a couple of days. Seductive smells of kipper and roast meats made us persevere with a particularly solid metal bin. Eventually, when we both leapt at it together from a nearby wall, striking it near the top with our combined weight, the thing toppled over and rolled down a concrete slope with an ear-splitting clashing and banging that awoke the entire neighbourhood. Lights suddenly beamed out from all directions, blinding and confusing us. Angry shouts further disorientated us and, pursued as we were by every dog in the place, we were lucky to escape with our lives.

After that incident we selected only plastic bins for our attention, but we still faced the danger of dogs. We could never be sure that one of them would not give the alarm while we were in the middle of the operation, forcing us to flee for our lives. Even when we did find a well-filled bin that was easy to raid and no dog around to disturb us, I can't say we ever actually enjoyed rooting through the contents. It was not that our efforts went unrewarded. Champ had not exaggerated about the amounts of good food thrown away by humans; we could easily have filled our stomachs daily on what we found in bins. But we, who had always eaten in peace and comfort from clean bowls, found foraging in dustbins sordid and degrading. We always stopped the moment the edge of our hunger was blunted, sickened by the jumbled mess of dirt and food and rubbish, much of it smelly and half-rotten. What to Champ was a triumph, was for us an unpleasant necessity of survival. And because we no longer enjoyed our meals, we grew steadily thinner; and because we were too unsettled to wash properly, and there was no-one to brush us, we grew daily less sleek.

What with the reconnoitring, the scavenging, the pursuing dogs, being shouted at by humans and dodging the things thrown at us, we also became bundles of nerves. We had problems too in finding safe places to sleep that were also dry and warm. We slept with one eye always open, fearful and shivering. Consequently we were always tired. With not enough time for rest, we had even less for thought and reflection, and none at all for race memory and cats' sacred duty and all the things we believed life to be about. We felt we had descended into an altogether low level of existence, far lower than any cat had the right to fall.

It was at this stage of the Odyssey, when our spirits had sunk to their lowest point, when life seemed hardly worth the living, that light appeared out of the darkness in the form of Mimi, the Jersey Cow.

Actually her real name, as it appeared on her pedigree, was Annabelle 111 of the Herd of Butterfold Riggleswell. But as she herself said, no-one could be expected to come out with all that razzmatazz tacked on to a simple 'Good Morning', so she was always known as Mimi.

It was something of a shock to find ourselves addressed by the head of a creamy brown cow regarding us from over the hedge, along the foot of which we had been cautiously and dejectedly proceeding. 'Hallo you two, are you lost? Can I direct you somewhere?' the head asked. The kindness of the voice and the soft look in the great lustrous eyes gave us courage to stand our ground and not bolt for cover.

'We don't know if we are lost because we don't know where we are going,' we replied.

'Lost or not, you look to me like two cats who could do with a rest and a nice refreshing drink of milk,' said Mimi. 'It's nearly milking time now, and I see our cowman coming to take us to the milking parlour, so why don't you follow us, and when he's finished I'll be free to entertain you.'

We hesitated just a little over accepting this invitation, for to tell the truth, although Dido and I are country cats born and bred, until our wanderings we had not had much to do with farm animals. All the creatures in our birth place had been pet animals, and anyway, we were too young then to have had anything to do with them. There had been sheep, geese, cows and chickens round about at Fairfield, but apart from sheep, we had only observed the others from a distance. The nearer fields where we hunted were all arable, mostly down to hay. Only when the hay was cut were animals allowed in our fields. It was always sheep who came, and then we hunted elsewhere because sheep intimidated us. We wouldn't even go for walks with Meg and Bill through a field of sheep. Our humans couldn't understand it, for the sheep ran away from them, but we had only to appear inside the gate for the whole flock to bunch up tightly together and advance upon us. They would loom over us like a solid white woollen wall that smelt strongly of grease and was set about with sideways moving jaws and strange sideways staring eyes. The wall never spoke, only loomed and moved those jaws and inched forward, ever closer; it was unnerving.

It was not until we ran away that we began to realize just how sheltered we had been in our self-contained world of Fairfield. In the lovely enclosed garden with the rich pickings all around we had never needed to roam far to find all we wanted. The only other creatures we ever talked to (and that amounted to little more than a 'Good Evening' or 'Lovely weather') were solitary badgers and foxes passing through on their nightly foraging. We had in truth led protected and insular lives.

In spite of our unfortunate experiences with sheep, however, we did not hesitate very long over Mimi's invitation, for huge though she appeared to us, she also seemed gentle, and was very well-spoken. There is a special quality about some creatures that inspires confidence, and this was the case with Mimi. We followed her at some distance, cautiously keeping to the shelter of the hedgerows. There were a dozen or so other cows also making their way towards a distant building, moving in a leisurely fashion, swaying decorously, but definitely not bunching like sheep. All the cows were coloured the same rich creamy brown as Mimi, and all looked very fine and special, as though they were something more than ordinary cows. Dido thought they bore a strong resemblance to illustrations of the goddess Hathor, the cow-headed bride of Horus. Close to they were even more handsome with delicate darker markings around ears and muzzles and with long lashes framing their beautiful large eyes.

The milking over, the cows passed us one by one where we sat waiting in the shadow of the milking parlour door. Mimi stayed behind, and after greeting us kindly again, she led us straight to a long slate slab where several large shallow dishes of milk sat cooling. 'These are fresh,' she said. 'They are put here for the cream to rise. Humans like to play about with our milk and make it into other things, but these bowls have not been tampered with as yet. Drink as much as you want,' she added; 'there is plenty more where that came from.'

'I can taste that wonderful milk even now; what a treat it was after the dustbin foraging and drinking from puddles. It was food fit for the most refined of our ancestors—cool, creamy, buttery and sweet, like no other milk I have had before or since, was it not, Dido?'

'I'll say it was. If we could have milk like that every day I would be happy to live on nothing else, except of course for a few choice mice and a tasty piece of liver now and then. But do go on, Sapphy, you've told the nasty part now and we are coming to the really good bits of the story.'

Mimi told us that the small pedigree Jersey herd, of which she was the matriarch, was kept by a rich human who reserved all the milk for his own use and that of his friends and neighbours. He didn't have to pasteurize it, a process of which Mimi thoroughly disapproved (so do we, now we know the difference) but kept it as it was, (which was why it tasted so delicious) and what was not drunk was turned into scrumptious butter, cream, yoghurt, cheeses, ice cream and other good things.

When we had had second and third helpings of this delectable and restorative food, Mimi led us to a sheltered sunny spot behind the cowshed where we could rest, and there she proceeded to question us gently about what we were doing roaming the fields of Middle England with no fixed abode. We told her our story and then, because she was so motherly and sympathetic, we found ourselves also telling her about how we had realized that we had done the wrong thing in running away, and that as a result we had lost our aims and purpose in life, and were feeling depressed and very unhappy.

'Well why don't you try and find out where your Meg and Bill have gone to, and go after them?' suggested Mimi. 'From what you say about them I am sure they would welcome you back.'

'We do not know where they have gone,' we replied. And Dido added with all her old fervour and with a pathetic little break in her voice, 'If we did know we would do anything to find them again.' I quickly chipped in before she could get too worked up, 'But it is impossible even to think about that now because we do not have a single clue about their whereabouts. We wouldn't know where to begin looking. Our only hope,' I continued, 'is that some other nice humans might one day invite us to live with them.'

'You are still very young,' said Mimi fondly, 'and clearly you had no idea of how lucky you were with your Meg and Bill. I doubt you would ever have the good fortune to find another such home, even if you were still small cuddly kittens. The world, alas, has all too few humans who are interested in the welfare of stray creatures, even in homeless waifs of their own kind. Many humans see other animals as nothing more than property to do with exactly as they please. As Champ told you, pets like you are often neglected or cruelly treated, and even abandoned. But you are perhaps unaware of how many other animals, both wild and domestic, fare even worse at the hands of humans? Take us cows for example. I don't think you can have any idea of the horrible things humans can do to us with their selective inbreeding, their growth hormones, genetic engineering, and the like? It is a huge and contentious subject that I won't go into now. Suffice it to say that there have been frightening rumours going around the country about a massive and unprecedented slaughtering of cattle because of a terrible brain condition. It is almost certain that this "mad cow" disease, as it is known, was inflicted upon us by humans themselves, probably through feeding us with the processed flesh and bones of sheep and other cattle. We are herbivores; we eat no meat, and certainly we are not cannibals to feed upon our own kind. But in order to serve their own short-sighted interests (which are nothing other than greed) there are humans prepared even to flout the laws of nature.'

'But please,' continued Mimi, 'don't let me give you the impression that we cows hate all humans, certainly not; there are many of the species for whom we have the warmest regard. Some, like our own farmer, treat us with respect and take good care of us, which is as it should be, since our relationship with humans goes back even further than yours does, little cats. In fact our ancestors were possibly the first creatures ever to live with man, and as you well-educated felines undoubtedly know, our Hathor was one of the foremost of the goddesses of the Egyptian pantheon. We are proud to fulfil our duty in the scheme of things. That even in death our bodies can be used to maintain life is a matter of satisfaction to us; it is a part of our role in the creation, just as much as it is for mice to be food for cats. But we think that we should become food for others only at the end of a well-lived and enjoyable life. We believe we have rights, like the right to good grass and clean water, to shade from burning sun and shelter from rain and cold. We think we should have the right to keep our young with us and suckle them and teach them; not have them taken from us to be reared by strangers, or fed from buckets while the best of our milk is taken for the humans' use. Most of all, we believe we have the right to keep our bull calves from the unbearable torture of being placed in narrow crates at birth, and kept there in the dark without being able to move until slaughtered, just in order that humans can feast on the unnaturally white baby meat.'

Mimi broke off her impassioned speech suddenly, with a 'You must excuse me, it is your predicament we are meant to be discussing, not my ideas for righting the wrongs of the world. I do get so carried away by the *Rights of Cattle*. When I remember the suffering and the terrible wasted lives of so many of my less fortunate sisters and brothers while I live so happy and privileged an existence here . . . But now enough of all that and back to your present problems. I have an idea that I might be able to help you poor lost little cats. From what you tell me, I feel sure you will only be truly happy again when you are back with your Bill and Meg, and I believe that you probably know more about where your humans have gone than you realize at present. You have been on the move constantly since you ran away, and your thoughts have been altogether taken up with questions of survival. If you could remain still for a while, somewhere secure (and I know just the place) so that you could relax and sleep and dream without having one eye always open for danger, you would probably be able to remember many things that would point you in the direction of your humans' new home.'

Whether we would succeed in remembering anything useful or not, the offer of peace and security and comfort even for a few hours was far too seductive to refuse.

What Mimi had in mind for us was a small hay loft above one end of a barn adjoining the milking parlour. A broad-runged ladder led up to it and sweet-smelling hay lay a foot or so deep on the floor. Mimi said that once, long ago, it had been the sleeping quarters of the cowman, but now the younger members of the farmer's family enjoyed camping up there on warm nights in their summer holidays. It was term-time at present, and the children were away at their boarding schools, so there would be no-one using it. We could stay there quite undisturbed; we would be able to come and go as we pleased and have as much milk as we could hold.

And that was how Dido and I found ourselves once again in the familiar world of dreaming our way back into our race memory and, of more immediate importance, into a world we had more recently left.

The first twenty-four hours in the barn were spent in deep refreshing sleep broken only for swift forays outside, for thorough and prolonged washing and grooming, and for leisurely draughts of milk from the wide bowls.

Dido has just pointed out that some readers who are knowledgeable about a cat's digestive system might be worried about the quantities of milk we appear to be drinking during this sojourn at Mimi's farm. Well let me hasten to reassure anyone who has fears on that score. Yes, we do indeed know that cows' milk can cause illness in cats, and we generally regard the delightful beverage as a treat to be indulged in only very occasionally. We certainly drank more of it at this point in our Odyssey than we would normally do, but probably not as much as it appears, because we took only small amounts at a time. That we suffered no adverse affects from it can probably be put down to the fact that we are large-framed felines and therefore able to eat and drink more than the average cat. 'There, does that deal with the subject Dido?'

Right, where were we? Ah yes, sleeping deeply and peacefully in the barn. We needed this time to recover from the rigours and pressures we had suffered since the Great Escape. Once we had caught up on sleep, however, dreams came thick and fast, and as we grew more relaxed we were able to focus our meditations more accurately. Soon we could get back to the world of Fairfield at will. We could roam through the garden, take cover in the tall grasses of the wild-flower meadow, perch on the fence posts to watch the wind making waves through the hay to reveal the scurrying mice. We could sit toasting ourselves in the huge brick inglenook beside a glowing log fire, or wait for our dinner besides the comforting Aga. And in all these locations were threads of speech to unravel as Bill and Meg exchanged remarks.

It is hard to tune in to conversations to which we have previously tried to shut our ears, these of course included all talk about the move. But we stuck to it, going over and over the same scenes, until the lost words formed and became audible to us: not all the words of course, only those that had entered our consciousness before we had removed ourselves from the scene. Fortified by discreet sips of the rich milk, our erstwhile scruffy coats groomed into a more acceptable state, we curled up in the warm scented hay. Heads on paws, tails tucked around us, eyes shut, we concentrated.

By the end of the fifth day, rested and sleek once again, we had amassed a large tangled web of seemingly unrelated fragments. Longing for a nice computer screen to organize these findings, we retired with Mimi to the sunny spot behind the cowshed, and scratched our 'Facts About the Move' in the warm dust of the yard. We sorted them out between us, as methodically as we could, in what we have learnt is called a brainstorming session. Dido was very good at this and took the lead.

'First, the house,' said Dido, eagerly writing with her paw. 'I think it is a small simple old farmhouse built of stone. Do you agree with that, Sapph?

'Yes, I do, a plain stone house facing north. I remembered them saying that it was a pity it was not south-facing. They also said that the huge views made up for everything—views of mountains and fields and trees, they said.'

'Definitely mountains all around,' wrote Dido. 'I think the house itself is on the side of a mountain. And it has a name,' she added thoughtfully.

'All houses have a name, Diddy,' I said, a little condescendingly perhaps. 'There is nothing special in that.'

'But most houses don't have names like this one, Sappho,' retorted my little sister, a touch snappily. 'This was a very strange name. Bill said it meant something to do with mountains and woods, but I couldn't read it.'

'Read it, Dido?' I queried sharply, startled out of my usual *sang-froid*. 'You mean you saw the name written down?'

'Yes, I did,' she replied; 'it was on the house agents' details pinned to the notice board in the kitchen,' said Dido. 'There was a photograph of the house and this name was written above it. There was another strange name I couldn't read underneath the photograph. That was the name of the village down the hill, Bill said. He couldn't read the name either; the letters were all wrong.'

She wrote down 'LLNWYLLEHCR' in the

dust. 'It was something like that, Sappho, something that didn't make a proper word in any language I know. The rest of the page was all right. I could read that. It was just like all the papers that came from estate agents at that time, all about room sizes and windows and things.'

I didn't remember this paper at all. I suppose I had closed my eyes to it along with so much else. All my clues had come from hearing Bill and Meg talking. I could remember them saying the house was too small, and that they were planning to build a bit onto the kitchen just as they had at Fairfield. There was something about a chimney too and a huge steel pipe that should have gone down it. I didn't understand that. Dido did though.

'I have that too,' she said. 'They were going to see if something could be done about putting the pipe down the chimney because it was an eyesore going up the outside wall. I expect it is a pipe for the Aga like there was at Fairfield. There was something about a spiral staircase too. I heard them say they were going to open up an old stone spiral staircase that went up beside the fire in the living room, so as to get rid of a modern flight of stairs that took up too much room.'

I was beginning to think that Dido was doing rather better than she had the right to as the younger sister, when Mimi broke in with her usual kindly diplomacy.

'Well done both of you,' she said, studying our list. 'That's a great deal of work, lots of clues there. Don't worry about what won't make sense, we can look at that later. Have you any more to tell while it is still fresh in your minds?'.

'Yes,' said Dido, more focussed than I had seen her in a long time. She wrote 'Second Category. The Surroundings—mostly mountains, farms, sheep and trees. Oh yes, and a steep narrow lane comes to an end just beyond the house. The lane leads up from a village, the village with the unreadable name that was written under the picture.'

I cut in quickly in order to maintain some credibility. 'And there is a town not far away too. It has a theatre and a cinema. Bill and Meg were excited about that because of Fairfield being so far from such things. Anything else?'

'Yes, five hours,' said Dido, scribbling furiously. 'Meg said she could get there in five hours. Bill said nonsense, it was more like six, even if you paid to cross the water. There was some talk about a barn too, not their own barn. I think someone else living nearby had a barn to put our furniture in, but I can't make sense of that, can you, Sapphy?'

I remembered how difficult it was at Fairfield when we first moved there with all the furniture piled up and getting in the way of the workmen. 'Perhaps they are leaving the furniture somewhere else this time while the builders are working on the house,' I said. 'You thought they were planning to have work done. But that is only guessing.'

'Yes, that must be it,' said Dido. 'I haven't got anything else yet, only scraps and words, nothing of use.'

Nor had I.

By now Dido's lists covered such a large area of the yard we were having to crane our necks to see it all. 'I think you have found out quite enough to get you started on your search,' said Mimi, sounding as pleased as though it was her own future that was at stake.

Now what part of the country do we think they were heading for?

A map of the British Isles was already propped up against the milking parlour wall. It had been in the hay loft, together with a lot of other school books that the children of the house must have left there. We had already located our beloved Fairfield and shed a tear or two on the page. But now, all useless emotions cast aside, we pointed out that as Fairfield was in the extreme south-east, with the sea very close, both to the south and to the east of it, a five or six hour journey could only be made in a northerly or westerly direction, or somewhere in the quadrant in between.

Together we studied the clues scratched out in the dirt of the yard, and pored over the map

144

until we came up with several possibilities. It could be the Lake District they were heading for because of the mountains and because it looked possible to drive there in five or six hours. The 'paying to cross the water' had also made us wonder about Ireland. It looked possible to get to a port in five or six hours because Meg is a very fast driver. But Bill had said 'even if you pay to cross the water' which implied you could also get to where they were going without crossing water, which is not the case with Ireland which is entirely surrounded by sea.

Could the water Bill had talked about be a river crossed by a toll bridge? The only big stretches of water that we could find which had toll bridges, and which fitted in with the driving time, was the Humber and the Bristol Channel. We ruled out the Humber because of industry, for we knew Tom and Meg's destination was very rural. That left the Bristol Channel, which suggested that Bill and Meg's destination could be Wales. Wales also had lots of mountains. It had stone-built farmhouses too, and sheep and barns and other things we had remembered from their conversations. But then so did the Lake District.

It was the crossing of the water that we decided was the most important point; Wales it must be. 'The strange sounding names would fit in with Wales too,' said Mimi, 'they speak a different language there from English.' Also, when we looked at the map again, we saw that Mimi's farm was on a direct line between Fairfield and the middle of Wales, and somehow we could not believe that this was just mere coincidence. The thought of Divine Intervention surfaced once more.

Having narrowed our search to Wales, we studied that part of the map again in more detail. Wales covered a large area and had a long coastline. We could not remember Bill and Meg saying anything about the seaside, so we thought the house would probably be away from the coast. There seemed to be mountains over most of Wales, the highest ones in the north. We thought we could safely rule out North Wales, however, because the route from Fairfield would not go there via the Bristol Channel. A lot of South Wales seemed to have towns and villages close together, which also did not fit in with the terrain Meg and Bill had talked about. So, in the end, after going through the clues again and again, we all decided that the middle part of Wales would be the most likely place to look.

'Congratulations my clever little friends,' said the warm-hearted Mimi when we had reached this point—although the congratulations were really entirely due to her. It was her kindness and forethought that had brought it all about.

'Perhaps a little more dreaming will make things even clearer,' she continued, 'but if you really intend to set out on this great Odyssey, I don't think you should delay your departure for too much longer. As far as I am concerned you could remain here for as long as you wished, indeed I have grown so fond of you both I would be delighted for you to make your home here. But you have unfinished business to attend to, and the sooner it is done the better. With winter coming on, I think you should get started within the next week or two. You don't want to encounter snowstorms on the way.'

But we were so excited at having found a sense of purpose again, a real goal to aim for, not to mention the possibility of being re-united with Meg and Bill, that although it was already late afternoon, we were minded to race off there and then.

Mimi tried to bring a little caution to bear. She pointed out that we still had a long hard road before us, and did not yet know exactly where our goal lay. We should rest up a little more and regain our full strength before setting out once again upon our Odyssey. In the end, she managed to persuade us to enjoy the luxury of one further night of comfort and security, one last good breakfast of rich milk and fat little barnyard mice before setting forth for the Bristol Channel and Wales.

CHAPTER NINE

THE WALL SPEAKS

It was a fine crisp autumn morning with steam rising from the flanks of Mimi and her sisters as they walked with us to the farm gate. Sapphy and I were very buoyed up now that our journey had a real purpose to it. With a meaningful if distant goal, and hopes of a happy outcome, it had indeed assumed the status of a real Odyssey. But in spite of all the excitement of setting out, and the anticipation of seeing Meg and Bill again, it was very hard to say farewell to Mimi. She had become such a dear friend to us as well as a timely saviour. She was our first real friend ever, apart from Sedgewick and Meg and Bill, and we felt very sad to think that we would probably never see her again.

Mimi, sensing our unhappiness, brought her head down to our level, breathing over us comfortingly with her warm breath. 'Well met little friends,' she said. 'Whatever happens we will always remember one other. Go now and be brave and full of fortitude, and everything will come right for you, I am sure of it. But if for any reason the Odyssey fails, and things to do not work out, there will always be a welcome here for you.' Our small noses touched hers, and in the next instant we had turned and sped off down the farm track.

Still following our shadows westward, we covered the ground swiftly, finding solace and delight in our renewed fitness and sense of well-being. Our thoughts to begin with were full of Mimi and the pleasant days we had spent with her. When we took our first rest beneath a hedgerow we found that we had both been experiencing the same sense of Mimi watching our progress from afar. It gave us courage, and made us feel we had to live up to her expectations of us. Mimi had been like a second mother to us, the first creature since Sedgewick to teach us new ways of looking at the world.

Self-sacrifice, forgiveness and service to others were Mimi's prime rules of life. She was able to see the good in everyone, and to bring out the best in them. It was not in our natures to be like her, but through her kindness to two scruffy dejected strangers she had made it possible for us to find our way forward, and we could begin to appreciate something of the meaning of her ideals.

It was through Mimi's example that we were able to face the full consequences of what our actions had meant to others. We now knew how unkind and unfair we had been to Meg and Bill. Even when we had been filled with anger at their making us leave our lovely Fairfield, we should have known that The Move was something they could not help; it was just part of their human limitations. We also knew that in spite of those limitations Meg and Bill had always done their best for us. And we, superior animals, whose sacred duty it was to influence them for the better, had repaid their care by running away and abandoning them. With a sense of shame we saw how horrid it must have been for Meg and Bill to come back to the car that day and discover we had gone. They must have thought that someone had catnapped us, or that children had undone the catch on the Kitty Kabins and frightened us into running off. They would blame themselves for leaving us alone. Perhaps they had bickered about whose fault it was, as Sappho and I had done when we were feeling low. We knew without doubt now that they would grieve over us, and that the excitement and pleasure of their new home would be spoilt by their worry about what had happened to us. Before our meeting with Mimi we would have said that this served them right. But now we felt mean and guilty, and these are not comfortable emotions to live with.

This was what Mimi had meant when she said that we had unfinished business to attend to. That business was to find Meg and Bill in order to set their minds at rest about us. Maybe we would die in the attempt. Maybe we would get there only to discover they were so angry with us that they did not want to have us living with them any more. But, whatever the outcome, we had no choice but to do our best to find them. Unless we made every effort to right the wrong we had done them, there would always be this burden of guilt, this stain upon our consciences. The whole basis of our role as true descendants of the high and sacred line of cats would be in jeopardy. No cat worthy of the name could live with that.

Fortunately, however, it was necessary to thrust all this uncomfortable and unaccustomed soul-searching to the back on our minds as we travelled onwards, for we needed all our concentration to avoid danger and to keep on course.

Since the map could not be carried with us, we had committed the relevant parts of it to memory, and had planned a route that would bring us eventually to the bridge over the Bristol Channel. We could not travel in a straight line, however, because of the need to avoid roads and towns, and to remain unseen. Whenever we changed direction to take advantage of a hedgerow or a friendly copse, we had to make sure we allowed for the deviation. It was not straightforward route-finding, especially as the only means we had of checking our whereabouts were the names on the occasional signposts we came to, names we might or might not have remembered from the map.

There were several terrifying alarms during the day when, out of woods or copses, came loud shouts and the sound of many feet crashing through undergrowth. This was followed by flights of pheasants bursting out of the trees. A splendid sight they made as they came sailing over the hedgerows with their long tail feathers streaming out behind them. But crouched besides those same hedgerows were men following the line of the flight with pointing guns. Fearful bangs were followed shortly afterwards by dull thuds, as the pheasants fell lifeless to the ground. Dogs ran out to pick up the limp bodies and place them at the gun men's feet.

We were dreadfully shocked for we had known several pheasants at Fairfield. They had paraded up and down our lane under the trees, and although we had never been exactly chummy with them, we had enjoyed their presence and admired the wonderful coloured plumage of the males. We had sometimes amused ourselves by pretending to stalk them, and if they had not been so large they might well have become our prey. But it was terrible to see them being killed like that in such numbers, and with so little respect. How could so few humans want to devour so many birds at once? It reminded us of those awful slaughters of lions that the Assyrians went in for. Records of these infamous and deplorable massacres can be seen on the stone tablets from Ninevah which are now in the British Museum. The poor lions are being let out of the cages, one at a time, and the Assyrian king, backed up by his soldiery, is demonstrating how brave he is by shooting each animal full of arrows just at the moment that the brave beast makes its bid for freedom.

I have heard humans say that cats are cruel too, that they torture their victims before they eat them. But this is just another example of human limitations, condemning behaviour and customs they know nothing about. For cats, as for other meat eaters, killing is part of everyday life. But as all life is sacred, a creature's departure from it requires rituals. We would not send any creature lightly to its death. The joy we feel at capturing our food is accompanied by respect for a prey worthy of us. We believe we celebrate life in death, and that what we eat becomes a part of us. We do not kill wantonly, except possibly the occasional shrew, and that is really accidental.

'Of course, Dido, whenever the subject of wanton killing is discussed amongst humans, they always cite the fox as the prime culprit. Do you think we should say something about that?'

'About foxes always killing every single hen in the hen run you mean? Yes perhaps we should. As you say, humans always bring that up to prove how mindlessly cruel other animals can be. Why don't you write about what that wise old vixen told us, Sapphy? My paws have done enough tapping for now. They feel as hot as if I had done a day's march.'

Dido and I met the vixen one night, early on in our Odyssey. Foxes had always been quite common at Fairfield, so we were not nervous when this one called out to us from under a large beech tree. We exchanged polite comments about the weather, and she suggested we join her for a rest and a chat. It was while we were talking about hunting and survival in the wild that the subject of multiple killings came up. It interested us for it is unnatural for any creature to kill more than it needs. The vixen said she had once got into a hen house at night and she had indeed killed every bird there. There was a stunned silence after she told us this, and we were so shocked and disgusted that we might well have made our excuses and left, had she not added, 'But I think I can explain why it happens.' And this is the gist of what she told us.

A fox that gets into a hen run or a hen house is pitched without warning into a scene of chaos and danger. The startled birds cannot scatter and run as they would in the open. In the confined space of the hut they flutter around desperately, their bodies crashing into one another and into the walls and against the fox itself. The air is filled with feathers and flapping wings. A terrible screeching rends the ears. Claws and beaks rend and tear. In the terrifying noise and confusion the clear distinction between predator and prey becomes blurred. It is as though suddenly the fox is fighting for survival rather than for food. The hens have become the enemy, not the prey, and the fox has to go on killing, fighting for its very life, until all the noise and commotion has ceased.

Dido and I have tried to put ourselves in the fox's position, to imagine being trapped in a close confined space with maybe rabbits instead of hens. It is certainly a very frightening scenario, and we think we too might behave in much the same way as the vixen in that sort of situation. Of course, the ones most to blame are the humans who confine their hens in houses that are not secure against foxes. No creature can be blamed for making the best use of her intelligence in order to get food, or for falling prey to her instinct for survival.

But back to the scene with the shooters. Even worse than our sense of horror at the slaughter was the fear that the dogs would scent us and chase us out into the open, where the men could shoot us. We dared not run, for the dogs were faster than us over open ground. All we could do was to stay where we were, cowering beneath the hedgerow, shaking with fear and losing valuable travelling time.

In spite of having to lie up several times because of shooters, by dusk we had made about fifteen miles, and had reached the outskirts of a village whose name we had committed to memory. We were relieved to be right on course, and warmed by the thought that Mimi would be proud of us if she knew. But we were very glad to drop down in long grass beneath a tree on the outskirts of the village, for we were tired out and our paws were hot and throbbing. Our fur was thick with dust from newly ploughed fields, and host to scores of burrs and thorns that had attached themselves to us when we had lurked in the undergrowth. There remained an hour to nightfall when we would be able to go in search of food; time for a well-earned rest. But, tired though we were, we remembered about the 'fortitude' Mimi had enjoined on us, and instead of sleeping, we spent the time grooming our coats. An hour or so later, feeling decidedly fresher, as one always does for a good wash, we set off on a dustbin-raiding run.

Half a hamburger, rice pudding scooped out of a half-full tin, meat ripped from a generously covered bone, some scraps of buttered bread and cheese and a lump of rather nice chocolate cake was our supper. Quite a pleasant meal it might have been if we could have eaten it at our leisure. But anticipating discovery at every moment, we bolted it down as fast as we could, and Dido was sick, as she so often is when she hurries over meals. We dared not wait for her to try again, but slipped swiftly and silently through the shadowed streets and out into the darkness beyond the village.

The night had become very cold. There was a fringe of bronze-coloured clouds around the moon; stars glittered icily and frost crackled around us. Where to go for shelter? We could see no buildings, likely or not. Fields and more fields stretched into the distance, with no shadow of a barn nor a single lighted window of a farm house. We were far too tired to make for the next village, so there seemed nothing for it but to curl up closely together under a hedgerow and shiver the time away until morning.

Dido was intoning 'Poor Tom's a cold, poor Tom's a cold', which was her current favourite line from King Lear when, to our shock, another and more sepulchral voice from the other side of the hedge said . . .

'Doubt you'll last the night out in that chilly spot.' A familiar greasy smell wafted over us. Sheep? But surely sheep don't talk; they just loom and move their mouths about, constantly in a circular motion. Remembering again Mimi's injunction to be brave, but at the same time checking that the hedge was thick and strong, we resisted the urge to run and instead, asked tremulously 'Are you a sheep? And were you talking to us?'

'Who else be there?' came the answer 'Course I be atalking to you, or rather we, the flock, be addressing you. Ain't you never bin addressed by sheep before?'

'No,' we said. 'We have been looked at by sheep, very closely in fact, but without a word being exchanged. We thought sheep just munched and loomed, and we were rather frightened because of being so much smaller.'

'Oh I see, you bin looked at. Well we sheep is cautious about whom we addresses. We takes our time. We likes to know who it is in our field, and being short sighted we have to get in close, and being timid we have to keep very tight together when we does look. And our mouths are always going around and around cos that is how we digests our food. But it don't mean we can't talk when we wants to, like just now when we was atelling you as how you'll freeze to death under that there hedgerow. Stiff and stark you'll be by morning.' At this last part of the speech Dido began mewing piteously. She is a brave little cat, but after the shootings and being sick and supperless, she had had more than enough trials for one day, and was quite overcome by the thought of being 'stiff and stark', as well as cold.

Her distress had an immediate effect on the unseen communicators behind the hedge 'Don't you take on so, little traveller,' came the strange voice. 'We don't mean you no harm, and no more will we let you freeze to death. You come on in here along of us, and we'll

159

keep you warm like you was tucked up in your own little bed.'

And that was how we spent the night, guests of a wall of sheep that had loomed over us, closer and closer, the ends of the wall bending around until we were in the centre of a circle, almost asphyxiated by the smell, but deliciously warm and comfortable between the soft fleeces.

'Shall I tell this next bit Sapphy? My paws have cooled down now, and we are coming to where you got your good idea. Since you are so modest, you won't be able to write about how clever you were, like I can.'

'All right Diddy, you write it, but don't waste too much time on lyrical descriptions. Stick to the conversation; that's what matters.'

'I'll try, Sapphy, but sheep talk is difficult. We never knew which one was talking. All the mouths moved together in that sideways munching movement. I think they were always conversing in unison like a Greek Chorus.'

'Of course they were, but that doesn't alter what was said does it? So do get on with it.'

'Right, I'll start at the beginning of the exchanges of confidences.'

As has been the way with travellers since the dawn of time, our kindly woolly hosts wanted to know our story, and their response to what we told them was very satisfactory.

'Well me dears, who would have thought it?' said the munching mouths. 'Such silky little creatures, with such soft little feet. And just the two of 'em alone against the world, yet brave they be as a couple of Big Horn rams.'

We were not sure that we approved of being compared with wild sheep, especially not with male ones. But the flock assured us there was nothing in all the world to equal the beauty and valour of Californian Big-Horns, and so we accepted the compliment in the spirit it was offered. The sheep were particularly intrigued about the part of our story that involved the escape from the car and they wanted us to tell them about it over and over again.

'If only we could do that, get out of a transport, what a triumph!' they bleated. 'We expects you clever little travellers knows that we sheep be the world's best escapers: it's what we lives for. We can get out of any field, given time. No matter how small a gap there be, we works at it, sharp hooves scraping away the earth, heads pushing at posts and stretching the wire. If it be too hard for a single sheep we lines up, one behind the other, shoulder to shoulder, leaning, until what was stopping us gives way, or until it moves enough for us to squeeze through, one after the other.'

A restless shudder ran through their ranks as they told us about their life's passion. Sappho and I had some difficulty understanding it. What was this fascination that they had with escaping? They didn't apparently want to go anywhere. In fact they said they were quite happy to return to their field again once they had got out of it. We decided it was just a harmless idiosyncrasy, and as they did seem to lead rather dull lives, it was probably a good thing that they had this outside interest. But there proved to be rather more to it than that.

'Escaping be our duty,' they told us. 'We be obliged to escape to show them there humans and their dogs that sheep be still sheep no matter what they do to us.'

They told us that they got very fed up with the image most humans had of sheep. And dogs were worse, they said, chasing sheep around the place just for fun, or just to show the humans what fine fellows dogs were.

'Even when we gets our one chance to be stars on the TV,' they said indignantly, 'who gets the credit for it? Why, just the men and the dogs! Twenty-five years that there *One Man and his Dog* as bin on the TV, and never a word of praise for us sheep. It's sheep as was doing all the work, running hither and yon through gates, and dithering about in shedding rings. Humans, pah! But stupid we ain't, and if they don't know by now why we needs to break out, we reckon as it's them as is the daft ones.'

Sheep ran their own contests for escapology, they told us. And the great prize was winning the Golden Fleece. This trophy was currently held by some Middle England sheep who had thought up a brilliant escape. One of their number had lain down across a cattle grid so that the rest of the flock could walk across the body to the other side and freedom. But they had never heard of sheep doing what Sappho and I had done, breaking out of what they called 'a transport'.

'If our flock could do that on the way to our winter pasture,' they said, 'we'd be famous. We'd be the new holders of the Golden Fleece for sure.' They bleated afresh with excitement at the thought.'

And that was when my sister, Sappho, hit upon her brilliant idea.

'Where is your winter pasture?' she asked.

'Wales,' replied the sheep. 'We sets off for there tomorrow.'

'Then I think we might be able to help you win your Golden Fleece,' said Sappho, quick as a flash.

My stomach was too empty for my brain to work at that speed, so I couldn't think what Sappho was on about. But what she had realized, of course, was that the sheep's transport was a heaven-sent opportunity for us to save time on our journey. That it was actually going to Wales was almost unbelievable good fortune. It would even overcome the anticipated difficulties of crossing the toll bridge.

The sheep had no objections to the plan. We were more than welcome to travel with them across the Bristol Channel into Wales. But as to helping them break out of 'the transport' they thought that was beyond the skill of any creatures, even such very clever little cats as Sappho and me.

I thought they might well be right. Sappho and I hated cars, and had never dreamed of entering one voluntarily. We had only experienced motor travel as captives penned in our horrible plastic Kitty Kabins. Where would we find the courage to go voluntarily into one of those huge slat-sided trucks we had sometimes seen near Fairfield, with sheep squashed in tightly all around us?

The sheep, sensing my hesitation, but not knowing the reason for it, urged us not to change our minds. 'Don't you worry little creatures,' they said. 'We'll look after you, even if you can't help us break out. No sheep never yet managed to break in or out of one of they transports. It'll be no disgrace if you can't find a way. It'll be a triumph for us getting you in. We knows exactly how to do that. Here's the plan. You'll have read your Homer, of course; all creatures knows their Homer. You recalls how Odysseus and his men escaped from the Cyclops' Cave? Well that's how we'll take you in, you hanging on under us, gripping our fur. That way nobody'll spot you.'

We were too ashamed to admit to the sheep that we were frightened of the truck. Actually that's not quite right. I was the only one struggling between shame and terror. Unbeknownst to me, Sappho had already overcome her fear of cars on the hard bitter ride from Fairfield when I had been unconscious. The only part of the planning that was worrying her was getting into the truck. Hanging on upside down under a smelly sheep was not an idea she relished. We couldn't talk to each other about these matters, however, since there was no possibility of private conversation enclosed as we were in the centre of the flock.

The sheep were too excited to sleep, and Sapphy and I were equally wakeful with thoughts of the morrow. We passed the night with the sheep entertaining us with their sagas and their sheeplore. We heard about the great sheep heroes of the past and about sheep in other lands that are never chased about by men or dogs, but are led from place to place by a man called a shepherd. 'Those sheep follows the shepherd because they chooses to. They knows as how the shepherd leads 'em to good grass and shade and water. We think they foreign sheep is lucky to live like that,' they said.

'My Mam told me it was like that here

once,' piped up a young ewe, the first solo voice we had heard amongst them. 'Sheep was led about she telled me, just like you said, by a good shepherd, and he didn't have no dog, and the sheep all wanted to go with him, cos they was like fond of him.'

'Sshhsshhsshh!' went the flock at this bold interruption. 'Break rank and speak for yerself, and see the mess you gets yerself into! There be no such thing as "A good shepherd". Shepherds be just shepherds. There be only one Good shepherd—"The Good Shepherd" we calls him. And he is huge and strong like a giant, only gentle too. And he travels everywhere, all around the world, gathering up all the sheep that ever was so as he can take them to the Good Green Pastures. We sheep knows he will come for us one day and gather us up, and while we waits, we keeps ourselves worthy of him by breaking out.'

'Why does breaking out make you worthy?' we asked, intrigued. 'Because,' said the flock with one loud voice. 'It means we still remembers what we be. It means that we knows as nobody owns us—much as they humans and dogs bosses us about. It means as we sheep still be free spirits.'

CHAPTER TEN

THE BREAKOUT

After talking so late into the night, morning
found Sappho and me very sleepy and
reluctant to stir from our warm smelly nest of
sheep. But we had some conferring to do, and
needed to clear our heads, so after a brief
stretch we sprang out over the backs of the
sheep and onto the white-rimed grass. It was
very cold.

'What are we going to do, Sapphy?' I asked,
as we ran to the other side of the field to get
our blood moving.

Sappho said that as far as she was

concerned, the chance of getting a lift straight into Wales was too good to miss. 'We must go with the sheep and help them as we promised,' she said. 'I know I can cope with the truck. What about you?'

I wasn't sure. In the face of Sappho's bravery I didn't want to confess how very scared I felt. So I said that perhaps if I thought about what Mimi had said about courage and fortitude I could go through with it. But as for helping the sheep break out, that seemed far too difficult a thing to me.

Sappho said not to worry about that as she had a plan already worked out. The success of the plan though would depend on how the tailgate of the sheep transporter fastened. 'We will have to get a good look at it before we get in,' she said, and just at that moment we heard the rumble of a heavy vehicle coming down the lane towards us. Soon a vast high truck with slatted sides had pulled up outside the gate to the field. Two men climbed down from the cab and went round to the back. We crept closer to watch them. The tailgate door was very solid with complicated fastenings. One of the men pulled out a large metal pin from the centre of a heavy rod which went the whole way across the back. He turned the bar, and we saw hooked pieces at the ends of it slide out of a pair of solid eye bolts. The full height of the tailgate then began slowly to bend outwards from the top under its own power. We watched it slowly and steadily swinging downwards, until the top of it touched the ground and formed a ramp. Behind it was another gate, not quite as solid as the first. This one opened in the centre, and expanded to make a fence on either side of the ramp. It all looked very technical and immensely strong; altogether a very daunting prospect.

'There is no way two cats and a bunch of sheep are going to get that open,' I said.

'I quite agree,' replied Sappho, quite unperturbed. 'We are going to have to think of something else.'

I rather hoped that meant she had changed her mind, and that we were not going to go with the sheep after all. But no, her busy brain was already working on an alternative plan. Telling me not to worry, she and I slipped back into the field to find the sheep who were to carry us into the transport.

I was thinking that this would probably turn out to be the unhappiest day of my life. And if anyone is thinking I was showing a lot less pluck than my sister, I might remind them that this was another instance of the effect of food on a cat's spirits. It was a clear case of how not keeping down a good supper the night before spelt the difference between buoyant optimism and gloomy acquiescence.

But back to the action.

It was a good thing there was no time to hang around worrying. The loading took every bit of grit I possessed. I only got through it by telling myself over and over that I must live up to Mimi's expectations of me. Sappho says she found this part tough too, even though she had been fortified by a good meal.

The problem, as usual, was the humans. The farmer and his helpers who had gathered for the loading had such low opinions of other creatures' intelligence that they felt they had to shout and swear at the sheep, and shout and swear at their dogs until all was panic and confusion. The dogs were barking and rushing around at a rate of knots, showing willing but achieving nothing more than chasing their own tails or giving the odd sly nip to a sheep's rump.

The large, and usually steady, old ewe beneath whose belly I was suspended was trembling so violently that I feared I would lose my hold on her fleece. She had already

170

been chased by the dogs in a dozen false directions. She had even tried to get away from the chaos by jumping over her sisters. By now I had a fair idea of what it was like to be riding in a rodeo, upside down on a bucking bronco. But in fact it was tenacity rather than courage that won the day, because there was nothing else we could do but hang on. If either of us cats had fallen off we would have been trampled to death by the hooves of the milling flock.

Sheer exhaustion eventually sorted out the confusion. The men lost their voices, the dogs gave up and lay down panting, and the sheep galloped unopposed into the transport—rather in the manner, I thought, of the Israelites fleeing into the dry passage across the Red Sea when they were pursued by Pharaoh's armies.

The sounds of those two formidable doors closing behind us, locking us in, was almost lost in the scraping of hooves as the sheep sorted themselves out and began to settle down. There was a general air of relief after the strain and panic of the preceding half-hour. Now that I was safe, I felt an unexpected surge of elation and adventure. We had done a brave thing like the heroes of old, like Odysseus himself, whom our ancestors had told Homer about. More than ever I felt myself in sympathy with the sheep, and as determined as Sappho to try and help them make their bid for the Golden Fleece.

The sheep's stampede into their transport had landed me on the top tier, very high above the ground, but able to see out and, more importantly, to climb out through the slats when I wanted to. Once the hooves had ceased their scraping I called out to Sappho who answered me from the bottom tier. We were both safely inside; the first part had gone according to plan. So far so good!

Before the sheep transporter started on its journey, the men who had been in such a hurry to get the sheep loaded, now seemed to have all the time in the world, and leaned on the gate talking, smoking and laughing. The dogs, still exhausted by their part in the proceedings, remained flopped on the ground panting, mouths open and tongues hanging out. This respite gave me time to join Sappho. It was not a difficult climb, and by descending on the side away from the men, I could not be spotted. The sheep watching my progress with interest were recovered enough to cheer as I crawled through the slats.

'Hark to they sheep,' said the farmer. 'Be in a right queer mood this morning. You take it easy with 'em, Bert, on the drive up. No use having them fretting and losing weight.'

'Right oh,' replied the driver. 'Suits me. Always ready to stop fer a cuppa. We'll take it easy, don't you worry.' And with that he and his mate climbed into the cab, and soon the moment I had been dreading arrived; the transport was on the move.

But strangely enough I found that being among kindly and admiring sheep, and able to take an interest in the proceedings, was not nearly so frightening as being on my own locked into my Kitty Kabin. When other creatures esteem you for your bravery, you can't let them down by admitting you are scared. Also Sappho and I had a lot of thinking and planning to do, and there is nothing like a job of work to prevent nervousness. Time was short, and the problem of the tailgate seemed insurmountable. How could our new friends break out from a truck that appeared as secure as any prison? To my mind the chance of winning the coveted award was fast receding.

We thought and thought and it was Sappho, of course, who was the first to come up with an idea. 'Mahomet and the mountain,' she said triumphantly. The rest of us, not being so well read in Muslim literature, just gaped blankly, so she added, 'When Mahomet found the mountain would not come to him, he had to go to the mountain. If we cannot open the tailgate we are going to have to get them to come and open it for us.'

'Which them?' chorused the sheep.

'Who?' I asked, more grammatical, but equally mystified.

'Why the driver and his mate, of course,' said Sappho.

'But why would they do that?' queried both sheep and I together; it seeming so improbable an action to us all.

'Well, actually, they might not,' said Sappho, 'but the way I see it is, if we can make them think something is seriously wrong with you sheep, they might open the doors to find out what the trouble is. The farmer told them you were behaving oddly before we left, and that might make them more likely to believe that something is seriously wrong. Unfortunately I can't think of a way of getting all of you out, those on the upper deck will have to stay put.'

The sheep said that would be fine, half a flock was better than none, and quite adequate for the purpose of winning the coveted Golden Fleece.

'My plan,' said Sappho, 'depends on you sheep being able to make the sort of noises that will cause great alarm. Do you think you can do that?'

'O yes,' bleated the sheep, giving us an example of a panic call on a high quavery note, 'we can act as if a fox or a stoat be got in along of us. Never you fear.'

'I shall also want you to drop down flat on the floor at the word of command,' said Sappho, and she went on to explain the whole plan. It was a bit complicated for the sheep to grasp, and had to be gone over several times, bit by bit. We had to get it absolutely right first time, Sappho told us; there would be no second chance.

We rehearsed our parts until we felt we could perform them in our sleep, and Sappho declared that we were as ready as ever we would be. Now all we had to do was wait for the right opportunity.

Quite soon after we had finished these preparations the truck rolled to a stop. Sappho nudged me, and waiting the required moment for the driver and his mate to get clear, I slipped out through the slats as planned, to reconnoitre. I had been chosen for this role because of the superb camouflage of my dark tabby stripes, and because Sappho had to remain at the command post.

We had stopped in a small lay-by alongside a very busy road, and it did not take long to see that it was not at all a suitable place for the sheep to break out. There were fields, but they were behind a high fence, and there was a deep ditch in front. In any case the stop turned out to be very brief, just time for the men to relieve themselves. We would simply have to hope that the next stop would be better suited to our purpose.

It was indeed. The next time we turned off the road it was into a large gravelled space with a transport café at the far end of it. Fields lay on both sides, separated from the car-park by only a shallow ditch and a low flimsy hedge which the sheep could easily charge through. This was it, I thought, and raced back to make my report to Sappho. She immediately went into action, directing her troops in their chorus of extreme distress.

The sheep were excellent, their cries and moans would have alarmed the most unobservant of humans, and indeed another driver just getting out of his truck looked hard at our transporter before going into the café. I followed him closely, and slipped inside with him as he opened the door.

'Who's driving the sheep?' he asked. Our driver said he was and why did anyone want to know? The other driver told him that the sheep were making a great commotion, and that he thought there must be something wrong with them.

'Oh no, they're alright mate, they're just a bit uppity this morning,' said our driver. 'Nothing to worry about,' and he turned his attention back to his plate heaped high with eggs and bacon and sausage that smelled so lovely it had me groaning like the sheep, only more genuinely, and for reasons of hunger.

And of course, the obvious happened, I was seen. For the first time when faced by strange humans I didn't run. I stood my ground, and my reward was scraps from every man sitting there. It was 'Here pussy, pussy,' and a bit of warm sausage would be dangled in front of me, or a generous slice of bacon would appear in someone else's hand. They competed with one another for the pleasure of seeing me eat their offerings, making remarks like 'There's a clever Stripey' and 'See she likes that' until I could eat no more, and sidled, rather shamefacedly, to the exit.

Sappho was not pleased by what she called my 'dereliction of duty' and 'fraternising with the enemy', but she had to agree that I had needed food, and that it was not in our nature to miss such an opportunity. What she was really upset about was the lack of response from our driver to the sheep's chorus of distress. She was no longer sure her plan would work.

It seemed an age before the transporter stopped again, and by that time we had all rather lost hope. I had been paying the price of 'fraternising with the enemy' by feeling decidedly travel-sick, a state not helped by the overpowering smell of closely packed sheep. When the transporter slowed down again and started to pull off the road, all I could think about was getting away from the foetid atmosphere and into the fresh air. Sappho, however, had her mind firmly on the matter in hand, and told me I was to follow the driver and his mate closely, but to be sure to remain unseen this time.

It was as well that I did follow closely, because the first thing I heard the driver say was 'Last stop before we unload Ted.' Last stop? Then this was also our last chance for the break out. I raced back to tell Sappho, and as I did so, I saw a flash of silver and out of the corner of my eye caught a glimpse of a wide stretch of water with a great bridge arching across it. We had reached the Bristol Channel, and Wales was within sight!

Sappho was calmer about both pieces of news than I would have thought possible. Turning to the crowded interior of the transport she drew herself up to her full stature. 'Sheep,' she said, 'this is the last chance, let us try and make it your finest hour.'

As I sped back towards the café to keep an eye on the humans, I could hear the swelling of a tremendous din of baaing and bleating and, glancing back over my shoulder, I swear the solid transporter was swaying from side to side.

The driver and his mate were at the counter ordering their lunch when the first human came looking for 'the driver of the sheep transporter'. 'What's up?' asked our driver. 'Not those bloody sheep again?'

'I think it's serious mate,' said the informant. 'There's got to be something wrong for sheep to making a din like that.'

Another driver on the same errand joined in the exchange. 'I quite agree,' he said. 'You better get back there quick and take a dekko, matey. The way that lot's milling about I'd say there's something's got in there with 'em, maybe one of them mink that's running wild.'

'Damn and Blast,' said our driver irreverently. 'Just when we was getting served. We'd better take a gander, Ted. Don't want to turn up with sheep with broken legs.'

Hurrah, it was working! Back I rushed at full speed to tell Sappho. I had a moment or two's grace in which to identify the best escape route, and then I laid low to watch. I heard Sappho giving her last instructions just as the driver and his mate arrived.

The sheep were in full cry as the humans started to lower the tailgate. It sounded most convincingly alarming, especially as the noise was now coming only from the upper deck. Below all was deathly quiet. As soon as the ramp was down, the driver and his mate sprung up and peered in through the narrow chinks in the second gate. ' 'Ere Bert' said the mate, 'they're all on the floor with their feet in the air. Come on, lets get this thing open and see what's up.'

You might think this was a silly thing for the men to do, and you would be right. But

Sappho's study of human nature has led her to believe that the stupid course is often the one chosen by humans when confronted by something out of the ordinary, and as is usual with cats, she was proved right.

No sooner had the driver unbarred the second gate, than the two parts of it burst open with the weight of fifty sheep, upright now, and using their combined strength to gain their freedom and scatter the enemy before them. If only they could have been waving banners, they would have looked like an avenging army, I thought admiringly.

I was all ready to lead them to the spot where they could charge through an inadequate hedge and gain the shelter of a grassy field. But to my horror the sheep ignored me and made straight for the road. Sappho, in hot pursuit, called for me to follow and try to head them off. From behind us came the cries of the sheep on the upper deck cheering their champions onwards.

'There's that stripey cat from the other café,' I heard the driver shout as I ran. ' 'Ow did it get 'ere?'

'And there's another one with 'er,' said the mate. 'Do yer reckon as its them as bin in the back with the sheep causing all this bovver?'

And then I was out of earshot and running hard alongside the pounding sheep, trying to persuade them to change course into the safety of a field. But there was no turning them. They kept straight down the centre of the road, and cars and trucks pulled into the sides to give them a clear passage. Sappho and I were level with the leaders as we clattered down the long slope towards the bridge, and as they ran they told us, between breaths, what they proposed to do.

They thanked us for our help, but said it was their escape now. They knew best what the flock had to do to win the Golden Fleece. Free spirits is what they were, they panted, and they were going to cross the bridge on their own hooves to prove it. Furthermore, they were going to take us with them, like the 'treasured little mascots we were', and bring us into Wales as they had promised. They urged us to jump up on their backs, as they knew we would not be able to keep up with their steady gallop for long.

By the time we reached the bridge, the police had arrived and had halted the traffic, which now stood stationary on either side for as far as the eye could see. The police themselves stood across the threshold of the bridge to bar our passage. But the thin blue line broke immediately before the onslaught of fifty determined sheep and two, we hoped (though in vain), inconspicuous cats.

As the sheep loped on down the centre of the bridge, drivers of the stationary cars watched them, bemused expressions on their faces. Some of them cheered. Some of them, as we were to discover later, took note of the two tabby cats perched aloft their woolly mounts.

The bridge was so long we couldn't see the other side until we came to the centre and began to descend the slope towards the further shore. The sheep picked up speed at this point, but still it seemed to take an age to cross, and Sappho and I, mere passengers, or rather mascots now, had time to look around and to observe the immense height we were above the waters of the Bristol Channel. We began to feel those awful stirrings of terror that cause cats to get stuck in the branches of tall trees. But it was indeed the sheep who were now in charge; all we could do was to think of Mimi, and to cling on all the tighter.

More police tried to halt our passage at the far side, but again the sheep didn't hesitate. As though already possessed of a greater glory, they went straight on through the middle of the road block with never a sideways glance. Nor did they stop until we came to a large white board at the side of the road which read *Croeso y Cymru* and underneath, *Welcome to Wales*.

Immediately on passing this sign, the sheep halted abruptly, left the road and, as though nothing at all out of the ordinary had occurred, began calmly to browse on the grass of the verge. Sappho and I were very glad to jump down and ease our muscles, stiff from the effort of hanging on to our gallant steeds.

This was where we parted company, and we had to be quick with our farewells for we knew that very soon humans would arrive to collect the sheep. Having aroused the suspicions of the sheep's truck driver, we thought it would be politic to make ourselves scarce.

'Well,' said the sheep, quickly making a wall around us for the last time, 'you've travelled along of us into Wales, and us sheep looked after you nice and comfortable, like was promised—even if the last stretch was on sheepback. The flock be all set for fame now. That award be ours, thanks to you two brave and clever little cats who only last night said as how they be scared o' sheep. Loomed you said, sheep loomed and munched. Well, you'll not be scared again when you be looked at by a flock. Sheep'll always be friends to you two cats on account of this day's work. You be free spirits like us, and coming from sheep that's as good as sharing in the glory o' the Golden Fleece.'

CHAPTER ELEVEN

INTO WALES

Dido is quite worn out with the pace of that last chapter. She re-lived the adventure to the full, relishing every thrilling moment of it—ardent as ever is Dido. And what a tale of daring and gallantry it was. Now that I am reminded of the sheer scale of it, I marvel that two cats, even of the direct and sacred feline lineage of Ancient Egypt, could have carried out so bold and intrepid an enterprise, especially when those same two cats are usually so shy and retiring. Travel did indeed prove an educational experience for us. We could never again be the naïve young cats who

184

set out from Fairfield all those moons ago. Like the wily Odysseus himself, facing perils and dangers had caused us to grow in courage, cunning and resolution. The only trouble with making journeys as far as we were concerned, was having to forego so many of the comforts of civilized living.

But enough of philosophizing and back to the action.

Our farewells to the sheep had been made not a moment too soon. Their transport came to collect them just as we had hopped over the hedge, and were heading off across the fields. We could hear it clearly above the roar of other traffic. The sheep on the upper deck were singing and cheering, celebrating the success of the flock. Their raucous happy songs of triumph made us suddenly and painfully aware that we were outside the camaraderie which we had so lately shared. Once again we were on our own in a strange country, feeling a little lost, lonely and apprehensive; suffering from reaction after all the derring-do. Now that the adrenalin of the action-filled day had ceased to flow, we also became aware of how very hungry and tired we were, I particularly so, not having had Dido's opportunity of gorging myself at a transport café. Another low point in the journey had come upon us.

Hardened travellers as we now were, however, we were not prepared to fall apart over minor miseries and hardships. We reminded ourselves of what an ancestor of ours had written not so long ago, in collaboration with Shakespeare—

'The west yet glimmers with some streaks of
    day.
Now spurs the lated traveller apace to gain
    the timely inn.'

No timely inn for us poor lated travellers, alas, but food being the immediate need, we too spurred apace to the top of the nearest hill in order to spy out the land.

Several small hamlets were in view in the middle distance, and making for the nearest of these, we arrived there just as night had fallen. About four or five small cottages were set back from a steep narrow lane, and our luck was in because the rubbish had been put out in black plastic bags ready for collection at some distance from the dwellings. Bags are so much easier to deal with than bins; a smart slash with a claw and the contents empty themselves neatly on the ground, ready to be picked over.

The first bag we investigated revealed a half-consumed joint of mutton which would normally have made us a good meal, but with our recent companions fresh in our thoughts it did not tempt us. Moving on to the next bag, we chose instead some scraps of bacon, half a hard-boiled egg, the remains of a tub of plain yoghurt (Dido has a passion for yoghurt), and filled up with the end of a loaf of wholemeal bread. No *haute cuisine*, certainly, but adequate travellers' fare.

Our sleeping quarters were on a slope of dry bracken out of the wind, and so tired were we that in spite of the cold night, I doubt a single whisker stirred between us, until the first gleam in the eastern sky awoke us to a new day. It being still too early for humans to be about, we considered it safe to return to the plastic bags for a quick breakfast. As Dido said earlier, it is not in a cat's nature to pass up the opportunity of a meal, and this particularly applies to cats on a journey, doubly uncertain of when their next meal will appear.

Fortified and alert once more we returned to our quest. We would follow a slightly new course now, north-west towards the middle of Wales. The countryside appeared very different from the England we had left, rougher we thought, and emptier, not so manicured, and somehow more challenging, more exciting. Small hills criss-crossed with grey dry-stone walls were often quite devoid of any dwellings, except perhaps for a small whitewashed farmhouse set down at random, it seemed, and reached by a ribbon of narrow winding road. It was country we could move through with ease because the main inhabitants were sheep of whom, of course, we would never again feel nervous.

There were lots of small woods and copses, and in spite of the lateness of the year, the hunting was not completely without reward. With the help of a little cautious dustbin raiding we were able to live off the land.

For three days we trotted on steadily, pausing only to hunt, scavenge and sleep. By the third night we reckoned we must have made some fifty miles or more. Our paws had hardened along with our ever-growing competence at survival techniques, and we felt lean and fit and altogether the seasoned travellers. If only we had known exactly where to go, where our ultimate destination lay, we might have been just as easy in our minds.

But the further we journeyed into Wales, the more worried we became about ever finding our humans again. In the euphoria of discovering the clues to where Meg and Bill had gone, we had planned no further than the crossing of the Bristol Channel. The rest, we realized now, had been left entirely to chance.

What had seemed so reasonable an

undertaking when we had talked it over with Mimi, now seemed wildly improbable. From the higher ground we were traversing we could see ahead of us range after range of mountains, the furthest blue-grey with distance. And no matter how far towards those mountains we travelled there always appeared further ranges of far blue hills. In so vast a canvas how could we hope to chance upon the one mountainside where Meg and Bill had made their home?

'We would have kept on searching for it though, wouldn't we, Sapphy? We would never have given up. We would have gone on and on seeking through those mountains, year after year if we had to, until we found them; if we had not met Arnold that is.'

'Yes, Dido, of course we would have. Our only other course would have been to 'Despair and Die', and I dealt with that in an earlier chapter. It is something cats do not do! But why the interruption? Who is supposed to be writing this chapter? You told the whole of the adventure of the Great Sheep Breakout without me commenting once, and now you have to be the one to introduce Arnold. It is not fair.'

'I am sorry, Sapphy. I didn't mean to muscle in on your turn. It is because you are such a good story teller. The picture you painted of how sad we were at that stage of the journey was so vivid that it was like living through it all over again. I was remembering that awful feeling of desolation when we thought we would never be able to find Bill and Meg. I just needed to be reassured that we would never have given up the search, that's all.'

'All right, Diddy, I do understand. But no more interruptions, please, unless I ask for them.'

Since Dido has jumped the gun about Arnold, I had better make the introduction without further ado.

Arnold is a large white Persian cat who caused us quite a shock when he suddenly jumped out in front of us, and said 'Dido and Sappho, I presume.' I corrected the presumption and said, 'Actually, since I am the elder, it is Sappho and Dido.'

But that was merely an automatic response on my part. For when it fully dawned upon me that this stranger, this striking white fluffy cat, had addressed us by name, I was speechless.

'Sorry if I startled you,' he said. 'The name's Arnold. Been following you for a while. Wanted to make sure it was you. Gosh, you do go at a fair lick, I'm quite puffed out.'

'But why are you following us, and how do you know our names?' we asked, completely bewildered.

'Oh dear, I suppose you must be completely out of touch. I hadn't thought of that,' said Arnold, mystifying us still further. 'Then let me be the first to tell you. My dear young

190

ladies, you are famous. There have been pictures of you and messages about you on the internet for weeks. You have been the main subject of Cat Forum since you disappeared from your humans' car all those weeks ago. Your latest exploits have even featured on radio news bulletins and television, as well as making the national newspapers—well the tabloids anyway. I don't think the broadsheets were prepared to risk such an unlikely story.'

This speech succeeded only in further baffling us. But Arnold continued unperturbed, full of enthusiasm.

'I recognized you from your pictures on the internet,' he said, 'and I am most honoured to meet you.' At which point he courteously extended a paw to each of us. 'I do hope you will consent to be my guests at the feast my friends are preparing for you at this very moment.'

Since we were still no wiser, and were certainly not prepared to go anywhere, even for food, until we had unravelled what this strange but gracious cat had to tell us, we remained seated, leaving Arnold no choice but to sit down with us, and attempt some elucidation. It was as well that he was a courteous and a patient cat because getting his extraordinary story straight took a great deal of time. Our proverbial feline curiosity made it necessary to go over the whole of it until all the threads fitted, and there were no loose ends left to tie. The recounting of it now, when we know all the facts, is very much simpler.

It appeared that from the very day we disappeared, Bill and Meg had set about trying to find us—strange we had not thought of that; it would have been such a comfort to us had we known. Meg had contacted the police, the RSPCA and the Cats' Protection League, and had put up many notices around Middle England, offering a reward for our return. None of these measures had elicited much in the way of direct response, except for the first sighting of us at the mobile transport café in the lay-by.

The kindly cooks had indeed told the RSPCA about us, and Meg and Bill had been informed that two cats answering our descriptions had been seen not far from the car-park where we had disappeared. From this tiny snippet of news our humans knew that we were still alive, and not in the grip of unscrupulous catnappers. Little comfort though this offered, apparently it had been enough to keep alive their hopes of finding us.

Bill had the idea of publishing our disappearance on the Cat Forum, a facility on the internet which we had never come across during our own surfing. Actually we had never had time for chat lines. Arnold however, a formidable computer buff who knew far more about the internet than Bill, said we hadn't missed much as the Cat Forum tended to be a rather soppy type of interchange between humans who liked to make sentimental small talk about the cats who lived with them. He and his friends just used it for lost and found cat notices, and it was there that Arnold had first come across us. He had immediately filed the notice of our disappearance on the Cat's own Cat Forum, CCF for short, which is a purely feline facility that humans cannot access because it has a code so clever it defeats the most determined of hackers [Hackers. Persons, usually humans, who try to break into other people's computers.]

Apparently our adventure had appealed to all computer-literate cats nation-wide, and each fresh report of us was eagerly awaited. Various sightings of us crossing Middle England had led to the view that we were making a planned journey, and soon there was speculation on the CCF about our destination. As our route continued westward some cats guessed we might be attempting to rejoin our humans. The more sporting types laid wagers on the likelihood of our succeeding.

The mounting interest in our progress had changed to intense excitement on the day of the Great Sheep Breakout. The first report came in early in the morning from a farm cat who had been following our progress on the internet and was on the lookout for us. She was probably the sole creature to have spotted us clinging on beneath the sheep as they were driven into their transporter. This echo of Odysseus and his men escaping from the Cyclops' cave appealed strongly to all the feline internet users.

A second report came from a cat at the transport café where the ravenous Dido had been seen by everybody. Some humans had also reported this sighting on the ordinary Cat Forum. The cats, of course, were monitoring both programs. All the computer-literate felines were now agog about what we were up to. They knew something very unusual must be afoot, but couldn't guess what. Again there was a great deal of speculation and a few wagers.

The Great Sheep Breakout came as a total surprise, but no cat on the CCF doubted for a moment but that it had been a carefully orchestrated escape plan, brilliantly conceived and impeccably carried out by two exceptional cats. As report after report flooded in, especially about us crossing the suspension bridge on sheepback, there was a general consensus that the event must be marked in some way. The decision was unanimous. Arnold said it had been decided to award us the highest honour that can be given to cats by cats. The Order of the Raised Paw was to be ours.

'There have been so many cats out looking for you since you crossed over onto Welsh soil,' said Arnold, 'it is a wonder you managed to escape detection for three full days. But I am very glad you did, and that it was I who eventually found you. Perhaps some of your glory will rub off on me. And now you have the story straight, and I have brought you fully up to date, let's get to my place and begin the feasting.'

Arnold had told us he lived with a very kind and laid-back human named Jack, who did not in least mind how many of Arnold's computer-buff friends came to visit. Jack was away working most of the day, and liked to think that Arnold was not lonely in his absence. There was no chance of that. Arnold's popularity with feline computer buffs was assured and not just because of his natural chumminess. Jack's computer was a particularly fine one with a huge memory, and was kept permanently on for receiving faxes. This meant that it was available for Arnold and his friends to use throughout the day while Jack was away, a very rare facility and one to be envied; like most other feline computer users, Dido and I have always to wait until the humans are in bed before we can get on-line.

A veritable crowd of Arnold's friends, assorted in colour, shape and size had gathered to greet us. Each of these cats came up to us by turn, solemnly raised a right paw, and touched us on the shoulder, murmuring greetings and congratulations the while. At this shower of praise and honour, Dido and I felt quite overwhelmed, and would have bolted, had the door not been firmly closed.

Our reaction was not to be wondered at really. Apart from our dear old Sedgewick and the brief encounter with Champ, the only other cats we had met since leaving our maternal home had been the huge fierce black tom who might, or might not, have been our Papa, and the horrible degenerate and unfriendly cats who had attacked us at Fairfield. We must have known, of course, that there were decent cats in the world, even some of the High and Sacred Line, like us. But our lives had been so secluded at Fairfield that, until this moment, we had had no opportunities for socializing, other than with Meg and Bill. And here we were suddenly surrounded by friendly, intelligent beings of our own race, all eager to sing our praises. Coming on top of Arnold's revelations about our new and far-flung fame, it was enough to unsettle any cat.

'I am sorry to interrupt again, Sapphy, but I have just thought of something important. Do you remember when we started writing this story long ago, when we were still quite young, and had just discovered Meg's writing machine? You wrote "We will tell our story and become famous." Well, we had no idea then that we were going to have all these adventures, and get given awards and things, did we? So how did you know we would become famous?'

'I was thinking of ancient times when I wrote that line, Dido, times when cats shared the fame of the human storytellers they worked with, as they did with Homer and Chaucer and Dr Johnson and Shakespeare, to name but a few. But as we had decided we could tell our own story ourselves on Meg's computer, I thought we would be famous as the first cats to go public. I certainly never dreamed of anything as exhausting as making an Odyssey. And as to becoming Cats of the Noble Order of the Raised Paw, even a feline of the direct line could not imagine that much fame and glory.'

But you are making me digress again. Back to the story.

Fortunately food was the next item on the agenda, and food overcomes shyness as nothing else can. A great feast had been prepared, the dishes of which were so numerous and so varied that I cannot remember them all. I know I ate sardines in so delicious an oil that it almost eclipsed the memory of the milk at Mimi's farm.

'Is that all you remember, Sapph? I know I had ham and chicken and steamed cod and prawns and egg mayonnaise and . . .'

'Yes, Dido. And I remember having to be very firm with you about slowing down before you were sick again.'

'Alas that is true. I never seem to learn that my stomach can't keep pace with my appetite. Eating is always a pleasure of course, and when it is as good as that feast was, it is a very great pleasure indeed. I wanted to make up for all the days of short rations. But it was a lovely feast wasn't it, Sapphy? and nobody really needed to bolt the food, because there was plenty for everyone.'

'But the best thing about the day was being with the other cats, don't you think, Diddy? The conversation, the jokes, the *esprit de corps*; all the warmth and camaraderie we had noticed among the sheep, and between Mimi and her sisters were ours too at last, and we revelled in it. We were amongst our own kind, not only accepted but the centre of attention— and that is always very gratifying. I know I lived my moment of glory to the full. We still need our privacy of course, but after that day I have rather changed my mind on the subject of cats needing their own space all of the time.'

When the feasting was finally over, and every cat replete and purring, Arnold took us to the computer and called up the Cats' Forum on the internet, so that we could see the entries for ourselves. And it was true that the majority of them were in the 'cute little pussy' mode that makes all proper cats seethe and fume, and which shows how little most humans know or guess about feline natures. The amiable Arnold, however, thought we were being too hard on them. He said the sentiments at least showed that these particular humans were very fond of their cats.

Bill's bulletin about our disappearance was brief and to the point, but because it was from him, we found it very poignant. It included a photograph of Dido and me, taken when we were very young with our arms around each other's necks, also very moving. But, more importantly, it heralded the end of our Odyssey, for Bill's e-mail address was included in the message, and from there we knew it was but a step to finding his postcode, which would unerringly lead us to where our humans were living. It was the best gift we could have received.

In fact our new computer buff friends had already done all this for us. One of them who knew the Welsh language was even able to tell us that the unpronounceable name meant the High Place. They showed it to us on the map, and we could see that it was about seventy miles away, in a very rugged part of Wales.

We then read the many replies to Bill's

notice of our disappearance. Most of these were recent, and to do with us having been seen on the bridge, riding on sheep amid a monumental traffic hold-up. Even on such a serious subject as lost cats, many of the messages employed such whimsy as 'Could these be your two little pussies riding home on woolly ponies?'

After we had all laughed our fill over the sillier of the exchanges, Dido and I were initiated into the code of the Cat's own Cat Forum, the CCF. Reading all about ourselves and our doings there was most interesting. We were impressed with the many accurate sightings of us, and the factual reporting of the cat users—no whimsy here, only informed conjecturing about our intentions. We had had no idea that our journey was being so well documented. What a useful tool Arnold and his friends had set up for their fellow cats. Never again would Dido and I feel cut off from our own kind.

When we were once again in a position to have regular access to the internet, the CCF would enable us to keep in touch with our new friends, as well as making it possible for us to communicate with like-minded cats in other countries. But, at this stage, we had little idea of just how powerful a force this world-wide network of cats could prove to be.

To end the celebrations on a suitably hilarious note, Arnold produced the tabloid newspapers which carried reports of The Great Breakout. One of them had a whole page taken up with a fuzzy picture of us riding sheepback across the bridge, and we could see that the photograph had been retouched to make us look bigger and fiercer. The headline above it read:

HAS THE BEAST OF BODMIN GIVEN BIRTH?

and in smaller letters underneath

Hell Cats Terrorize Sheep into Fear-Crazed Stampede

Another had

PLAGUE CATS AT LARGE ON SEVERN BRIDGE

And a third read

NEW SUPER CAT THREAT TO MOTORISTS

There was even an interview with the driver of the sheep transport, an exclusive it was called. It was very good, all about these devilish cunning cats who had planned to steal the sheep and murder the driver and his mate. It said that a Hollywood horror film company

201

had made an offer to buy up the rights.

The gist of most of the stories was that some fierce, cat-like creatures, of immense size and ferocity, had been savaging a flock of sheep, and bringing fear and chaos to 'innocent motorists'. One imaginative report said that the creatures had been trying to drive the sheep into the Bristol Channel—like the 'unclean spirits entering into the Gadarene Swine and rushing into the sea', suggested one cat, amid hoots of laughter.

There were lots of creative embellishments about savage snarling and dripping blood and huge teeth and claws ripping into the sheep's flesh. Most papers had got the right bridge, however, and the fact that there were just two of us feline monsters, but, for the rest it was pure invention and very funny. We could not think why Bill and Meg did not read such papers, and enjoy a good laugh instead of wading through the unwieldy broadsheets they favoured.

And thinking about Meg and Bill, and of how we used to lie full-stretch on their newspapers to prevent them reading and make them play with us instead, Dido and I, suddenly and at the same time, felt an overwhelming need to take our leave of all these friendly cats, and get on our way. It would take us the best part of a week to cover those seventy miles, and now we knew exactly where we were going, and how close we were to our humans, further delay was unbearable.

'Hang on a minute,' said Arnold. 'You don't mean to say you propose walking straight up to the front door and presenting yourselves to your humans, just like that, without any sort of warning? Why the shock could be enough to give them a heart attack.'

As we had thought of doing exactly that, and had anticipated nothing other than a joyful reunion, we were somewhat taken aback that Arnold thought so little of the idea. As his guests, however, we felt obliged to listen to his argument. For his part he was clearly trying to put what he had to say into diplomatic language.

'Perhaps you have been on the road so long,' he said, 'you have forgotten what humans are like. But just think for a moment. If you arrive at Bill and Meg's doorstep on your own eight paws, especially after all the strange sightings of you on the internet and in the tabloids, they will have to face the fact that you (dumb animals as they have always supposed you to be) have powers and intelligence they never even dreamed of. At the very least, they will realize that you have somehow been able to work out where they had gone, and then follow them through a great tract of country that was unknown to you. Do you really believe they can face that sort of knowledge? I know that my Jack could not, and he is a particularly open-minded and unflappable member of the human race. Remember, man thinks of himself as the most, if not the only intelligent species on the planet. I know it is our task to bring humans to a better understanding of the world they inhabit. With our help they might one day even master more subtle means of communication, and begin to learn from the more developed intelligences of other creatures. But until that time arrives it would surely not be wise to present your humans with irrefutable proof of your superior brainpower.'

It was true. In our eagerness to be re-united with Bill and Meg we had forgotten the cardinal rule—'Humankind cannot bear very much reality.' By arriving under our own steam, we risked shaking the very foundations of their world. No, of course we could not do that to them, turn up unannounced on their doorstep. We had to behave strictly within the bounds of their expectations of cats. We had to let them think of themselves as being in control.

'I have a plan you might like to consider,' said Arnold quickly, before we had time to feel too deeply disappointed at not being able to race off immediately towards our goal. And he proceeded to outline a very sage and suitable solution to the dilemma.

An hour later all Arnold's friends had returned to their respective homes. The computer was locked onto the Cat Forum, with Bill's message about our disappearance on screen. Dido and

I, posed as we were in our portrait, were awaiting the arrival of Arnold's human.

A key turned in the front door, and Jack, a large, plump jolly-looking man with a pleasant rosy face came in and said, 'Hallo, Arnold old chap, been having a good time with your pals? Don't think I've met these two before, have I? Well let's see if there are any messages. Hallo, what's this on the screen? I don't remember leaving the Cat Forum up. Have you been walking over the keyboard again, Arnold? Hey, wait a minute, Missing Cats? Surely I have seen these two before . . . ?'

And of course there we were, the missing Sappho and Dido, right at his feet, our arms around each other's necks, just as we appeared on the screen.

'I say, Arnold,' said Jack, after gulping once or twice, 'unless I am very much mistaken, these visitors of yours are the two lost cats that some poor chap's been looking for for weeks. Fancy them turning up here . . . and the message on the screen at the same time . . . talk about coincidences!'

And he looked very hard, first at Arnold, and then at us. Finally he shrugged and said, 'I suppose we shall never get to the bottom of it. It will remain just one more item on the growing list of "things unexplained". But I had better put this poor chap out of his misery right away, and let him know his pets have turned up safe and well.'

CHAPTER TWELVE

ENDINGS AND BEGINNINGS

Later that night, while Arnold was initiating Dido and me into some of the finer points of computer technique, seventy miles away Bill turned on his computer and found there was e-mail awaiting his attention.

News of the Great Sheep Escape had reached Bill days before, together with the various speculative items on the Cat Forum about two tabby cats who had been seen with the sheep. He had not dared to imagine that those two free-booting cats could possibly be his own long-lost Sappho and Dido, but secretly he had toyed with the idea, and his hopes of finding us were therefore raised.

Even before he brought Jack's message up on the screen, he had a hunch that the message would be something to do with us; at least that is what he subsequently claimed on the many occasions we heard him recalling the details of our return. Jack had included his telephone number in the e-mail, so upon reading the message Bill was able to contact him immediately and confirm that it was indeed 'his very own Sappho and Dido' who had been found safe and well.

In their first flush of joy and excitement at the news, Meg and Bill had thought to jump immediately into their car, and drive over and fetch us. It was only when Jack pointed out that it was really very late for such a long difficult drive over twisting pot-holed mountain roads, and on such a dark and blustery night, that they agreed to wait. Jack said he had to come their way on business the following day, and assured them that it would be no bother at all for him to bring us with him. We of course knew that this was all part of Arnold's carefully thought-out plan to spare us the indignity of ending our Odyssey as penned prisoners in the plastic Kitty Kabins. Arnold seemed able to manage Jack perfectly; and we decided we would study his methods, so as to acquire a similar knack in dealing with Meg and Bill.

So it was that we were able to arrive, still

more or less under our own control, at the new home. Arnold enjoys what he calls 'going for a spin', and he accompanied us in order to point out sights of interest along the way, and also to make sure that the reunion went according to plan. Jack's luxurious car, in which we were left free to stretch out on the sumptuous seats and gaze through the windows, gave me a totally new glimpse into the pleasures of motoring, and I could see why Arnold enjoyed it. Dido alas could not; she felt just as travel-sick as she does in any vehicle. Fortunately she was able to hold out long enough to spare the fine leather upholstery.

Where we would have travelled on foot in a straighter line, winding through the river valleys on tortuous single track roads was a slow business, and it was only after several hours that Jack stopped the car at the foot of a steep narrow lane for a final check on directions. And there above us, perched high on tree-clad slopes, we saw a small grey stone building that caused Dido to catch her breath. Low and flat-fronted, with small windows, a chimney at each end and a central door, it was as simple as a child's drawing; it was also unmistakeably the house Dido had seen in the picture pinned to the notice board at Fairfield. High Place was a most appropriate name for it, as we could now see. In front of the house were two figures, tiny with distance, but instantly recognisable as our humans, Meg and

Bill, looking out for our approach.

When Odysseus got back to his home on Ithaca, he had a fight on his hands, but our Odyssey ended on a very different note. Having Jack and Arnold present at the homecoming, of course, made it considerably easier for everyone. If cats could ever be said to have any sort of failing, it is that of dealing with displays of emotion. We easily become embarrassed and overwhelmed by effusive outbursts of any kind, and it is really best to leave us to make the first overtures. It is the same when humans have been away from home for any period. To come rushing in after their holidays and expect their cats to respond immediately to cuddles and protestations of affection is unrealistic. We are not like dogs, passion bursting out all over the place. We experience things just as intensely as any creature, but we are chary about laying bare our souls in public. A reunion taking place on strange and alien territory, of course, presents further complications, as I think we mentioned earlier.

Returning Prodigals though we were, with hearts both contrite and full of joy at seeing our humans again, we could allow ourselves no more than a brief twining around their ankles before going through the Proper Rituals For Arrival at a Strange Place—a procedure in which we were by now well versed. First and foremost, it means a thorough inspection of the house and grounds. It is our responsibility to make sure that no dangers are lurking, and we can trust no-one else with this task. Then all entrances have to be located, together with all possible hiding and lurking places. All emergency exits must be memorized.

Only when these basic duties have been thoroughly carried out is the scene set to sample the subtle vibrations of the place. This is a process that can take many hours, days, weeks even. But compromise is necessary too, and on special occasions, such as this one, we can allow ourselves to gain just a general impression before submitting to being the focus of attention. Even then, of course, a suitable distance has to be maintained.

To give them their due, Bill and Meg have now grasped these cardinal rules concerning cats, but in such a charged situation they, like all their kind, have a tendency to forget, and to let their feelings take over. Social duties—making coffee for Jack, providing refreshment for us and for Arnold, and talking—about cats and their doings of course—gave our humans something concrete to occupy them, and allowed us time to adjust to being together again.

The real moment of reunion came in the evening, after Jack and Arnold had departed. A log fire was burning on the hearth with Meg and Bill settled in their chairs beside it. Dido and I, by now fully orientated, jumped up into their laps to be stroked and petted and fussed over, while we nuzzled and rubbed against them, purring our contentment until we thought our hearts would burst. After all our wanderings we were back where we truly belonged. Now we knew absolutely and for certain that home was where our humans were. The 'unfinished business' had been well and truly completed, and Mimi, we knew, would be overjoyed when the news reached her.

That was the beginning of our new life in the Welsh Hills. All very moving and satisfactory of course, but a great deal of adjustment on our part was still required before we would feel truly settled.

Meg and Bill had fallen in love with The High Place because of the views, but for us those same wide expanses were at first a touch too spectacular. High though the house was, behind it the land rose in still higher ridges, terminating in dark bare peaks that dominated the landscape. Stark implacable shapes with clouds masses rolling over them, these mountains presented an awesome presence; altogether too intimidating we found them.

In front of the house, the land fell away more gently, through innumerable small green fields edged with thick rough hedgerows. Fine tall trees dotted the landscape down to the valley bottom with its broad swift-flowing river. On clear days we can see right across this valley, and on and on, over range after range of hills, for sixty miles and more, in a great sweeping arc from the east to the west. Dido and I, reared in the gently undulating lands of Kent, at first found the peaks and the wide spreading views almost as alarming as the mountains behind. Nothing, not even our adventurous journey, had prepared us for the sight of huge red kites and buzzards, and even aeroplanes flying below us. It made us feel most uncomfortably exposed, visible to every living creature.

Perched on a narrow ledge at over a thousand feet above sea level, and almost at the limit of the tree line, we were also at the mercy of winds which blew around the house with sufficient force to knock an unwary cat off its feet. Winter was already upon us when we arrived, and on bad days rain, sleet and snow came driving horizontally across the hillside, straight at us. Venturing outside under such conditions was an act of pure heroism.

The most effective way to cope with this inclement environment was to grow heavier and to cultivate a thicker coat. Eating more was no problem to either of us, and we quickly gained sufficient weight to keep us earthbound. But my beautiful silky fur has never provided as much protection as Dido's more serviceable woolly coat. By the end of that first winter, considerably rounder and with a dense, blanket-like covering, she made a very useful buffer to crouch behind.

We were also rather surprised by the state of the accommodation at Ty Uchaf. Although we had been on the road for six weeks, which should have been ample time for Meg and Bill to get the place comfortable, much of it was in a state of chaos. Nearly all our furniture was in a neighbouring barn, and a gang of builders was milling about the cottage creating further chaos, and commandeering what few chairs there were for their lengthy tea breaks. '*Déjà vu*,' do I hear you say? Yes indeed! except that this Welsh house, being built of huge blocks of stone, compounded the noise and the dust of each and every job most dreadfully. A fearsome angle grinder and an equally clamorous cement mixer never ceased their chorus from morning until night, and what with the wind and the rain and the exposed views, it all seemed far worse than the previous move. By the time The High Place was fit to live in, we reckoned any debt of penitence we

213

owed our humans had been more than worked off.

Fortunately conditions improved before our patience was strained quite to breaking point or our tempers spoiled for ever. On the wonderful day when the builders finally departed, together with their loathsome noisy tools and most of their mess, it seemed sufficient bliss just to bask in the sudden peace and quiet that filled the cottage. Further joys followed swiftly. The last of the dust and mess was cleared away, and our furniture was brought out of the barn, appearing piece by piece, like familiar old friends. With all our remembered chattels about us once again— pictures on the walls, rugs on the flagstone floors, soft lighting replacing naked bulbs, cushions, curtains and comfortable chairs—life took a new turn.

An unexpected bonus made the biggest difference of all to us; this was the window embrasures. We had thought the walls of Ty Uchaf were three feet thick because anything less and the place would have blown down long ago. Now we discovered that these massive walls also provided wonderfully deep window openings with low expansive sills. Cleared of all the builders' clutter that had previously filled them, the sills offered perfectly positioned places from which a cat could observe the world. The thoughtful provision of double glazing and thick soft cushions on the sills meant we now had eight separate vantage points in which to lie at full stretch in warm draught-proof comfort, and take in the surroundings without exposing ourselves to the elements. Lapped in this tasteful pleasant luxury, we too could at last begin to enjoy the great sweeping panoramas that are such a feature of Ty Uchaf.

These window seats have remained our favourite indoor places, and when we have had enough of watching the birds, cows, sheep, rabbits, foxes and all the other creatures who live around us in this wide and gracious valley, and are satiated with the grandeur of the ever-changing skies, the far blue hills, or of the mists rising from the valley floor transforming the world into a still sea with only the tops of the peaks rising out of it like islands, then we can face inward to the snug oak-beamed, fire-lit interior, dangle our paws over the warm air rising from the radiators, and return to our dreaming.

'Sapphy, I thought it was supposed to be me who did the lyrical descriptions?'

'*I*, Diddy, not *me*,' '*I*, who did the lyrical descriptions. But yes, you are right, I have gone on a bit, haven't I? Why did you not stop me?'

'Well actually, Sapph, I was rather enjoying it, especially the bit about the mists in the valleys being like the sea. I love those mysterious mornings too; they remind me of

Japanese paintings I've seen on the internet, the same simple brush strokes and soft subtle shades. And what about the sunsets? You didn't mention those wonderful long summer evenings with the sun sinking redly behind the long ridge.'

'Careful now, Dido, don't you get side-tracked too. We are supposed to be summing up our experiences, and bringing our Odyssey to its close, not writing purple prose. Arnold says he wants our manuscript in by the end of the month, so he can begin publishing it in instalments on the CCF. He wants to get the reaction of other cats as to whether the time is ripe for making our story available to humans. He is not at all sure that they are ready for it yet, at least not in all countries.'

'You know, Sapphy, I find it hard to get used to the idea of Arnold being such an influence in the world. Apart from that startling mass of white fur, he seemed such an ordinary and unassuming cat when we first met him. Do you think perhaps we were too preoccupied with our own affairs then to realize what an exceptional feline he really is? And yet he is not even a tabby, so he cannot be in the direct and sacred line, like us, can he?'

'Well all cats must come from a common African ancestor of course, just as humans think they do. Arnold told me that his forebears were taken to Persia in the sixth-century BC, and that it was there they

216

acquired their long fluffy coats. He also told me how they came under the influence of Ahura Mazda, and took on various Middle Eastern beliefs and ideas, which is why his race memory differs from ours. Not that any of that bears any direct relation to his present position of power, of course. That comes from him being the right cat in the right time and place. As we suggested to Shakespeare:

' "There is a tide in the affairs of cats which taken at the flood leads on to fortune." Computers gave Arnold the opportunity to extend his influence and he has seized it. Creating a cats' own web site, that was secure from human infiltration was a stroke of genius: the CCF has a membership of millions of cats world-wide now, and growing all the time. As the head of so vast a network Arnold is indeed a power on the international scene. What a good thing he is also such a dear amiable old fellow. A human with such a force at his command would be tempted to take over the world.'

'Perish the thought. But then despotism is no part of a cat's nature, is it, Sapph Sapph? We leave that strictly to humans. I don't think any cat cares more about the unity of creation and the cat's role in promoting harmony than Arnold does.'

'He would certainly like to hasten on the day when the curse of the Tower of Babel is broken, when every creature speaks with a single voice, and when humans can once more communicate with the rest of creation. In the meantime, he just seems keen for all cats to get on with what they are best at—being benign influences. The CCF helps a lot in this, of course, by sharing ideas, which is why Arnold has been urging us to buckle to and get this book finished.'

We don't write as much or as quickly now as we did in Fairfield. This is partly due to the CCF, which has certainly changed our lives. The time we spend on the internet now, talking with cats who are eager to exchange ideas with the latest members of the Order of the Raised Paw has given us a new confidence. From being the social misfits of Fairfield, we find ourselves widely respected members of the feline race, and we like that very much.

Many of the exchanges are also very challenging, and have opened our minds to new ideas and other race memories. Dear old Sedgewick would have approved of that. The 'University of Life' he would have called it. It has also made us question what we once thought we knew, and Sedgewick would also think that was all to the good. Remember how he used to say 'A question answered is a subject closed. While a good question is one that leads straight to another'?

Had our affairs worked out as we wished them to, had we been able to remain in our self-contained paradise of Fairfield, we would have become ever more insular and inward-looking. At best we would have continued to be simple keepers of the records of the ancestors, bearers of our race memory and nothing more. Not that we have deserted race memory, no indeed, it is still our basis and remains at the heart of our dreaming. But no longer is it a fixed and static source. Together with our cat consciousness, it is dynamic and continually expanding—rather like those internalized maps of our territories. I recall something else Sedgewick used to say, it was that nothing ever remains still; it must either grow or decay. 'Past and future,' he said, 'exist only in the present, and the present lasts no longer than a single breath, in and out.'

All of which, of course, means we have forfeited our certainties, our hard and fast beliefs about life, death and the universe. We live with risk now, prepared to explore new ground, and to be proved wrong. It is all a little frightening and uncomfortable, but far more exciting—just like our Odyssey proved.

But we don't spend all our time on philosophy and dreaming and the internet. Our social life has become far richer too, and we enjoy friendships we would never have dreamed of at Fairfield. We keep in touch with all the friends we made on our epic journey. An intricate network of communication always existed in the animal kingdom aeons before computers were thought of, and messages pass

219

to and fro by the old procedure, especially in this remote spot. In this way we hear frequently from Mimi, who remains ever the same, always on the lookout for any waifs or strays who need a little mothering and some good advice. One day we plan take a trip back to her farm, and enjoy some more of that lovely milk.

Champ, the cat tramp who was so surprised to learn that there were humans who could be kind, has had a change of fortune. Soon after we met him in the woods of Middle England, he was offered the chance of a home with a lonely old man living in a run-down cottage in the woods. Because of what we had told him Champ found the necessary trust to give co-habitation with humans another try, and recently we heard that both he and the old man are very content with the arrangement. We gather that the old man had also been a tramp for many years, so the two would have a lot in common. Apparently Champ brings his human regular gifts of rabbits.

The vixen who tried to explain the dilemma of mass slaughter in the henhouse also got news through to us by way of a feline user of the CCF whom she knows. She wanted us to share her triumph in surviving the local hunt for yet another season. She also gave us news of Fairfield, which has not changed much, we gather, except that the countryside around is being progressively ruined by hedgerow clearance and the destruction of some of the fine old trees we knew. The vixen thinks she too might soon move on.

We even heard directly from Fairfield one day. The new owners have a cat sharing with them now, a computer-literate young feline called Target, who surfs the net regularly, and whom we have recruited to the CCF. It was strange hearing from him about our lost paradise, stranger still to realize we no longer mourn its loss, and that even if offered the chance we would not return there. That brought us up sharp, making us realize how much fuller and more enjoyable we are finding life here in these Welsh hills.

Strangely enough, however, it is with sheep that news travels fastest. We had not been here for more than a day or two when we were visited by one of the local flocks. Sheep rule in Wales: there are at least a hundred of them to every single human, and although sheep cannot at present obtain direct access to the internet, they have a very efficient grapevine of their own. We saw this particular bunch looming in a very determined way around our perimeter fence. With our recently acquired knowledge of the ways of sheep, we were able to wait patiently until they were ready. When they had loomed sufficiently they addressed us, in unison as usual.

'If you be the two cats as helped the flock with the transport doors,' they said, 'we was to tell you the award is won.' We replied that it had indeed been our doing, and we thanked them for the news, which indeed made us very glad and proud of the part we had played in the affair.

Two hours later we were still at the fence, for the sheep were very reluctant to stop talking. Eager to give us all the news of the valley, they were equally keen to find out all they could about us, our humans and all our doings. Gossips they most certainly were, and of an heroic capacity, but kindly with it. There was no malice or spite in their chatter, only harmless fun coupled with an insatiable inquisitiveness. We believed them absolutely when they said every sheep in the valley would be a friend to us because of what we had done for their kind.

It was this friendly meeting with the sheep that gave us the spur to go beyond Ty Uchaf's fences, and to begin exploring our new and infinitely wide domain. At first we took advantage of Meg and Bill's daily walks, and they rather liked us coming with them, though they did not really enjoy waiting for us to catch up. We soon realized we did not need their protection, and that it was more fun to wander around at our own pace, stopping when we wanted to, changing tack and making diversions at will, or even walking for a while with other companions.

It was with some young sheep that we made

a memorable trek to the top of our very first mountain. What a dizzy exhilarating expedition that was. We had thought the cottage was as high as we would ever wish to be, but it is nothing compared to the experience of having infinite space on every side, and of feeling that at any moment we might sail off into space like two furry balloons. The summit seemed to us a place where only gods should walk, and we could imagine that the fierce wild wind was punishing us for our temerity in being there. Yet our woolly friends were nibbling away at the sparse turf as though they were nowhere at all special.

Our local sheep are particularly laid back, and rather grand at the same time, possibly because their farmers are awarded a double subsidy for keeping them; 'or is it a triple subsidy, Dido?'

'I think it is three, Sappho, one for being a sheep, a second for being a hill sheep, and a third for being a Welsh hill sheep.'

Whatever it is, the flock told us that Welsh hill sheep have to make a very special effort to remember that it is their duty to escape, and to demonstrate that they 'Do still be free spirits' and remain worthy of their Good Shepherd. Spending nearly all the year roaming at liberty on the open hillsides where there is all the liberty they want, as well as plenty of cover and sweet and varied grasses, they tell us they feel not only free but privileged. Also on the hill there is nowhere for them to break out of, and so there is very little chance that these sheep will ever win an award for escapology.

It is only on the occasions when they are brought down for lambing, dipping, shearing or whatever they are forced to put up with, that they have the opportunity of making any sort of protest. They certainly make the most of these infrequent gatherings, however, and are driven down the narrow lanes to the pens accompanied by such a racket of bleating and baaing, such attempts to break away through impossibly small gaps; such jibes and rude remarks to the bewildered dogs that we, watching their progress from one of our vantage points, find in hard not to offend them with our laughter.

Lambing time is when the sheeplore is passed on to the next generation in these parts. Every ewe makes a point of taking its own lamb on a breakout before they are let out on the hills again. But there is no passion or derring-do attached to these expeditions, such as Dido and I observed in Middle England. Their hearts are not really in it; they are too content.

Other local friends, cows, ponies—both wild and tame, badgers, foxes, fellow cats, also tame and feral, all stop to pass the time of day with us whenever we meet. We even have human friends here who know us by sight and will stop and stroke us if we let them. Our lives in what we used to call 'Post The Fall' are so much richer for these daily contacts, that now at last we understand why Meg and Bill were so unhappy in Fairfield, and why they set such store by neighbourliness and the importance of saying 'Good Morning'.

We are very proud of our Meg and Bill for having had the courage to up sticks and leave the lovely but poisoned paradise of Fairfield. And we think them very clever to have found this haven in the hills. They are working very hard now to make the place as civilized and as catworthy as our former Eden. All that tree-planting and those nice thick hedgerows are already making a great difference to our comfort and security. We do our best to encourage their efforts, even when it is only vegetables they are sowing, in which of course, we have no interest. We sit beside them, just out of harm's way, as they mow the lawns, as they dig and hoe the hard neglected ground, as they rake the seed beds, or lever out piles of great stones from the soil. It all looks like very hard work to us, and we could almost wish that the enemy of our youth, the gardener, was here to help them. But they seem happy enough to be doing it themselves, and we read that it is good for humans to be out in the fresh air 'eating bread by the sweat of their brow.' Sometimes we think that it is like being back in the very beginning of things, when our ancestors first made contact with those early Ancient Egyptians, digging and delving in the rich black silt of the Nile Basin. So immensely long an association of cats and humankind! Quite nostalgic it makes us feel. It also makes us sorry that we did not trust Meg and Bill to do the right thing by us, and that we caused them such grief and worry by running off.

Nevertheless, we do not regret our Odyssey. We cannot, for had we allowed ourselves to be brought here penned and protesting, unwilling prisoners, then anger and bitterness would have clouded our vision, and it would have been a different place that we came to. Besides, the Odyssey itself was an important part of our development as cats, as we hope we have been able to show.

We have never discovered just how much our humans knew or guessed about our journey. We think they suspect far more than they are prepared to admit to one another, or even to themselves. They still occasionally talk about it, as they did that first night, going over what they see as the many strange coincidences surrounding our disappearance and re-appearance so close to The High Place. We sometimes catch them looking at us very speculatively, as though to say 'If only cats could talk'. What irony, when we so long for them to do the same!

'But, Sapphy, don't you think Bill and Meg have already come a long way since we have lived with them? They are certainly much happier and far more perceptive. I even hear Bill making remarks like, 'It could be that animals are a lot more intelligent than we give them credit for.'

'Yes, Dido, I do agree, they are growing more discerning, and are certainly much more contented. But it is very slow work, isn't it? Speech and the written word are still their only real means of communication. They have no notion at all of direct contact, mind to mind.'

'Well, I have heard a rumour, Sapph, that humans have finally got round to making thought-responsive computers. So some of them seem to understand the principle. I can't wait for Bill to get one, if only to give my paws a rest. Just think, Sappho, we could write stories without even having to open our eyes.'

I have heard of it too, and I can see that such a computer would be wonderful for all sorts of creatures who cannot use a keyboard, but how our humans will cope with it rather puzzles me. No matter how hard I concentrate, I can seldom plant a single thought into either of their heads, even when I stare straight at them for minutes on end. I have only just managed to teach them to recognize simple requests like "milk", "I want you to come out in the garden with me, now", or "I want to be brushed" and "You are sitting in my place, please get off". But the rudimentary sounds I have to use in order to express these requests only elicit a response after long and exhausting repetition.'

'Yes I know, Sapphy, and very noisy it is too. I think my method of scratching at a cupboard door or an ankle gets a quicker response, and is certainly quieter. But joking aside, you are right, any attempt at real communication is exhausting work with little reward as yet. Perhaps our book will make a difference, that is if Arnold decides it is to be published on the open market. I hope he does; it would be rather nice to do talks on the radio and make appearances on television and give interviews to the newspapers.'

'There are times, Dido, when I fear that fame has already turned your head. Do try to remember that mystery is a cat's chief strength. I cannot think television appearances would do much to enhance that, do you?'

'Sorry, Sapph, I was just joking. But seriously, do you think we will ever go travelling again; embark on a new Odyssey?'

'Well, personally, I hope not, not in the way you mean. I like it where I am. But of course life is full of journeys; every moment we are travelling, in thought, if not in time and space. Some journeys lead nowhere; some even go backwards and plunge off the edge into chaos. Many journeys are inevitable, as ours was— though few, of course, are on so heroic a scale. All journeys are risky, for there still exist no foolproof maps to guarantee success. But there are resting places along the way, gardens in the wilderness, like this one, where the traveller can pause and find delight, and glean a little wisdom and understanding before setting out again.

Eventually we all must come to the brink, and sail off in our astral barges along the Great Celestial Highway of the Stars, clutching in our paws our Book of the Dead. But who knows, Dido, if even that is the last journey?'

The End